Troublesome Angels and Flying Machines

'*Troublesome Angels and Flying Machines* is a charming and highly readable fancy' *TES*

'An impressive debut from Hazel Marshall . . . . this is old-fashioned fare in the best tradition of adventure stories, expertly paced and confidently written' *Sunday Herald*

'An inventive hoot, fast moving and quite bonkers' *Families SE*

'An entertaining and unusual story for younger readers . . . the villains are excellent' *History Teaching Review*

'An exciting debut novel . . . Intelligently written and a real page-turner.' *Birmingham Post*

Flying in and out of bookshops soon . . .

Troublesome Angels and the Red Island Pirates

Don't miss it!

Troublesome Angels and Flying Machines

Hazel Marshall

OXFORD
UNIVERSITY PRESS

OXFORD

UNIVERSITY PRESS

Great Clarendon Street, Oxford OX2 6DP

Oxford University Press is a department of the University of Oxford.
It furthers the University's objective of excellence in research, scholarship,
and education by publishing worldwide in

Oxford New York

Auckland Cape Town Dar es Salaam Hong Kong Karachi
Kuala Lumpur Madrid Melbourne Mexico City Nairobi
New Delhi Shanghai Taipei Toronto

With offices in

Argentina Austria Brazil Chile Czech Republic France Greece
Guatemala Hungary Italy Japan Poland Portugal Singapore
South Korea Switzerland Thailand Turkey Ukraine Vietnam

Oxford is a registered trade mark of Oxford University Press
in the UK and in certain other countries

British Library Cataloguing in Publication Data available

ISBN-13: 978-0-19-275442-4
ISBN-10: 0-19-275442-4

1 3 5 7 9 10 8 6 4 2

Typeset by AFS Image Setters Ltd, Glasgow

Printed and bound in Great Britain by
Cox & Wyman Ltd, Reading, Berkshire

For all those who believed

Prologue

Count Maleficio cursed as his cape swept a dish on to the floor. He sniffed. He couldn't be sure but it smelt as though he had knocked over a dish of pickled quinces. He stood still for a moment, listening to hear whether he had disturbed anyone.

Through in the other room, the old man turned over in his bed and mumbled but did not wake.

The Count waited a few moments to be sure. Then, wrapping his long cape more securely round himself, he crept over to the window. He banged his shin on a low chest and had to bite his lip until he tasted blood to stop a cry escaping him.

'What, what?' cried the old man. The Count froze. But the old man was only talking in his sleep. He lay quietly after his cry and the Count turned his attention back to the window seat. He slowly lifted the lid, wincing a little at the creak that sounded as he did so. He wished he had left this creeping around to his servant. Had he been caught it would have been no matter, servants being easy enough to replace. If *he* were caught it would be downright embarrassing.

Pulling a small instrument out of his bag, the Count placed it on his face. Suddenly he could see much better. The little glass roundels brought everything into focus. It was still dark in the room.

From what he could see there were a lot of things in the opened seat. The Count was looking for one thing in particular. Without light it was going to be difficult to find it. He debated with himself for a moment.

The Count felt the hairs on his back prickle to attention. He looked over to the other room but he could still see the hump of the old man as he lay in bed. He could also hear the gentle snores that the old man made. He shrugged off his belief that someone was watching him and made the decision to light a small candle. Once he had done that, it was quick work to find the papers that he wanted.

Chapter 1

'It's come!' cried Blanco, running down the *calle*. He tripped over the pig and lay sprawled in the dirt but nothing could shake the smile from his face. He turned over and grinned up at the sky.

His great-uncle came to the front door and looked down at where Blanco lay smiling in the mud. He prodded him with his cane.

'What are you doing?' he asked.

Blanco turned his head and gazed at him in excitement.

'It's come, Gump,' he cried, waving a piece of black parchment at him. 'My invitation!'

If Blanco hadn't been looking up at the sky so avidly he would have seen a small frown cross his great-uncle's face. As it was, by the time he looked back at him, his great-uncle was smiling with pleasure at Blanco's happiness.

'You'd better come in then.'

He ducked back into the house and, after a moment of brushing himself down, Blanco followed him.

'What does it say?' asked Gump, settling down in his favourite chair and pulling his blanket snugly around himself. He always claimed that old bones needed more covering than young ones.

Blanco looked around the room, spotted the honeyed

wafers that were always somewhere near his great-uncle, and sat down next to them. Cramming his mouth with two at once he handed the letter over to his great-uncle.

'*My dear Blanco*,' read his great-uncle, peering closely at the letter. It was on black parchment and the writing was in silver which made it a little difficult to read. '*It was a great pleasure to meet you during my last visit to Venice.*'

Here Gump lifted his face from the page. 'I wish I could say the same about him. He ate all my pickled quinces, you know.'

Blanco sighed heavily. This was a conversation that they had often. 'He didn't *eat* them, Gump. He knocked them off the table with his cloak.'

Gump grunted and returned to the letter. Pickled quinces were a great favourite of his. '*I was happy to view all your inventions. I was particularly impressed with your flying machine.*'

Here Blanco could not stop a self-satisfied smirk crossing his face and he crammed some more honeyed wafers into his mouth. He was quite impressed with his flying machine himself—even if it didn't actually work yet.

'They're mine,' his uncle said crossly, looking up. The tell-tale crack of the honey had alerted him to the fact that his wafers were in imminent danger of disappearing altogether. 'Bella made them for me specially.'

'Bella likes you,' said Blanco, calmly continuing to chew. 'She'll make you some more.'

His great-uncle blushed and quickly read on. '*I would like to invite you to my castle to view my own continuing experimentation with flying machines. I believe that if we work together we could come up with a working model.'* He put the letter down again. 'Well, that's quite exciting, isn't it?'

As his great-uncle read these words, Blanco leapt to his feet and ran round the room with his arms outstretched. Not surprisingly, he knocked over a dish.

'Oops,' he said as he bent down to pick the contents up.

'It was the pickled quinces, wasn't it?' Gump asked with a sigh.

Blanco nodded and giggled guiltily.

'I think you should think carefully before you go and see this man,' Gump said.

'Because I knocked over your pickled quinces?' asked Blanco.

'Well, he's already having an unfortunate effect on you,' said Gump, but he was laughing as he said it. 'No, I think—'

'I have to go, Gump,' Blanco interrupted. 'You know I do. It's everything I've ever dreamed of. And you know who's to blame for that.'

Gump sighed heavily. 'I should never have told you that story,' he said. 'It's all my fault, just as your father always says.'

'My father!' Blanco sank back down in the chair, seemingly at a loss for the words that he needed to sum up his attitude to his father fully. 'My father wouldn't know a good idea if one introduced itself to him.'

'He is a very successful trader,' said Gump mildly. 'He must have had a few good ideas in his time. And it is thanks to him that you met up with this Count Maleficio in the first place.'

'That's true,' said Blanco, lying back in the chair and remembering his first meeting with the Count. He had come to purchase some emeralds from his father and his father had brought him home for dinner. Over the meal the Count and Blanco had discovered a shared interest in trying to build a flying machine. Signor Taddei, usually so disparaging of his son's interest, had to listen with feigned enthusiasm since Count Maleficio had promised to buy more jewels from him in the future.

Blanco snorted. 'Well, I'm not taking over father's business, no matter how much he begs me. I hate it. It's so boring. Anyway, I've got much more important things to do.'

'Like what?' asked Gump.

'Like what?' repeated Blanco in disbelief. 'Like going to visit the Count and building a flying machine.'

'It's a long way away,' said Gump, shivering as though he found the idea of travel to be extremely distasteful.

Blanco stared at him incredulously. 'You went to China!' he exclaimed. 'Spain is leagues closer than that!'

'Yes, but I was gone for twenty-four years,' said Gump, smiling at the memory of his journeyings, his fingers smoothing out the rug over his knees. 'Do you want to be away for twenty-four years?'

'If I could fly,' said Blanco firmly, 'I would stay away for ever.'

This voiced wish hung in the air between them. Blanco could almost see the words forming as they came out of his mouth and as soon as he said them a part of him wished them back. He turned away and wandered around the room. He stopped in front of the silver girdle given to Gump by a Tartar knight. Next to it lay a gold tablet, a present from the Great Khan. His Great-Uncle Marco Polo (Gump to him) had travelled further than any other man had ever travelled. Many people did not believe that he had done so and so, to quieten their chattering tongues, he had written a book all about his adventures. At least, he had dictated the book while in prison, captured fighting the Genoese. It hadn't stopped the gossips but it had whiled away the hours in prison. Blanco sighed. His great-uncle had had such an exciting life. Unlike himself.

'It *is* all your fault that I want to fly,' Blanco said suddenly.

'I didn't mean to drop you that time,' said Gump defensively. 'It was an accident. I've told you so a thousand times.'

'Not that,' said Blanco. Gump had once dropped Blanco from the balcony while he was trying to explain to a visitor how big the desert was that he had once crossed. 'I mean the story about the kite man.'

One of Blanco's favourite stories in his great-uncle's book was of a man who was sent aloft on a kite to test the strength of the wind and thus the good fortune or otherwise of the voyage. Gump always maintained that the man sent up was either a fool or a drunkard and that nobody ever volunteered for the task. Blanco had always thought that if he lived in China he would have volunteered. In a similar spirit of experimentation, when he was younger, he had persuaded some of his friends to throw him out of the window of their tower, tied to some sheets and with long strings attached. He had fallen straight to the ground and had broken his arm. It still ached sometimes in damp weather.

Gump grunted. 'Well, I suppose a young man should have some adventures before he settles down. Although I wish it wasn't that Count you were going to see. I don't trust him.'

Blanco raised his eyes heavenwards. He hadn't realized just how much his great-uncle loved his pickled quinces.

'Perhaps if I came with you,' continued Gump. He looked at Blanco as though waiting for an invitation. None was forthcoming. He sighed. 'When will you go?' he asked.

'Soon,' said Blanco.

'Will your father agree?' asked Gump.

Blanco said nothing.

'No.'

'But, father—'

'No.'

They were sitting at dinner. His father sat at the head of the table. His sister, Angelica, sat on his right and his mother on his left. Blanco sat facing his father from the bottom of the table. The table itself was piled high with lots of food. Baked fish in dill sauce, roasted beef cooked with spices, capon legs in milk and honey, to name only those closest to Blanco. Bella shuffled in between every course and placed yet more delicacies on the table. On her third trip in she winked at Blanco, trying to cheer him up. He gave her a weak smile in return. Fighting with his father left him with little energy for anything more than that. A large pig's head lay in the middle of the table, an apple crammed in its mouth. It looked as though it was screaming for help and the apple was stopping the noise. Blanco knew exactly how the pig felt.

Blanco opened his mouth again but his sister, Angelica, saw him and leapt in first.

'Why do you always come up with stupid ideas at dinnertime?' she asked him, in her high tinkly voice which made his skin feel as though it was too tight for his body. 'You know that father has a delicate stomach and doesn't like to be upset when he's eating.' She looked beatific as she spoke but the glance she threw at Blanco was more demonic than anything else. With her beautiful face and her long blonde hair everybody thought that she was an angel. Everyone except Blanco and Gump.

Signor Taddei patted his daughter's cheek affectionately and scowled down the table at his son. His eyebrows overlapped alarmingly. His frequently-referred-to delicate stomach never stopped him overloading his plate with meats and he gnawed away at them as he stared at his son. Blanco, in turn, looked pleadingly at his mother. She cast him a frightened look from under lowered eyelids and then helped herself to another piece of crackling pork. Blanco sighed. If his mother ate any more she wouldn't be able to fit at table soon. He addressed his father again.

Signor Taddei's eyes narrowed suddenly. 'This better not have anything to do with flying,' he said, pointing a capon leg at Blanco. The scorn with which he loaded the last word made his feelings plain. 'Every time you jump off the roof with those wings I am laughed at in the guild meetings.' He paused and leaned forward. 'And I don't like being laughed at.'

Blanco had said nothing about flying, merely that the Count had invited him to visit and he realized that he had been right to keep the flying part quiet.

'Gump says that every young man should have adventures,' he said.

Signor Taddei waved the capon leg angrily at Blanco and in his fury he did not notice that pieces of meat came flying out of his mouth with every word he uttered.

'That man is nothing but a liar and a charlatan. They don't call him *Il Milione* for nothing, you know. I wouldn't believe a word he says.'

'Why is it that they call him that again?' asked Angelica innocently, though she knew full well. She also knew that Blanco hated hearing their great-uncle slighted.

'That book!' spat out Signor Taddei. 'Not one true word in it. He never travelled to China or any of those other places that he talks about! He probably sat in jail for the entire time, or in some tavern making up tales. And I'm not the only one who thinks it!'

Blanco sighed. He knew that there were two camps in Venice—those who believed his great-uncle's tales and those who didn't. There was no doubt into which camp his father fell. And similarly there was no doubt into which camp he himself fell.

'So where did all those things in his house come from and the letters of recommendation from the Great Khan's court? And the golden tablet?'

'Bought them all from traders or forged them,' said Signor Taddei shortly. He turned on Blanco's mother who shrank back in her seat as far as her bulk would allow her, which wasn't far. 'I should have asked for a bigger dowry to take you on. The amount of derision I have to take on his account.'

'There's no need to blame Mama!' Blanco shouted, pushing his chair back. 'And I still want to know why I can't go to see the Count. He's a friend of yours after all!'

'Don't shout at me!' roared Signor Taddei, getting to his feet. 'I said no and I meant no! And he's not a friend of mine. He's a business acquaintance. And my business with him is finished for now so there's no need for you to go anywhere near him! Spending any time with you would put him off doing business with us in the future! No. You'll stay here and learn the business! It's about time you did some work for this family.'

'I could help while he's gone,' put in Angelica quickly. Blanco knew she wasn't doing it for his sake. She had her own concerns and none of them were for him.

Signor Taddei's face softened slightly as he looked down at his daughter but he shook his head. 'You're my little girl. Business is no place for you,' he said, not seeing the look of fury that crossed her face at his words. 'But you,' he pointed at Blanco, 'had better learn some enthusiasm for it or I'll beat it into you!' He stormed out.

'I hate you!' said Angelica, getting to her feet. 'If you weren't here, he'd have to teach me the business.'

'No, he wouldn't,' Blanco shot back at her. 'If I wasn't here, he'd marry you off to someone he *could* teach the business to.'

She slammed the door. Blanco looked at his mother. She looked at him and then ate another cake.

Chapter 2

Gump had introduced Blanco to Bartolommeo the map maker almost as soon as he could walk. He would take him to his shop which was always filled with a curious smell—a mix of spices, old paper, and, sometimes, if you faced the right way, a whiff of the sea—a combination which conjured up exotic and faraway places. While Gump and Bartolommeo would empty a few wine flagons, Blanco would trace various journeys across countries. Gump had shown him the journey that he himself had taken and while that one had enthralled Blanco for a time, soon he was planning his own trips, taking wild detours and unlikely leaps across seas and oceans. Gump and Bartolommeo would urge him on—the lower the level in the wine flagons, the more ambitious the adventures.

'Do you think I could sail round the world, Gump?' Blanco would ask and Gump would shrug his shoulders and say he didn't see why not. 'Just because no one's done it, doesn't mean it can't be done,' he would always say.

Blanco paused outside the shop door. He could see another figure in there with Bartolommeo. He wanted to check who it was before he went in. He didn't want word getting back to his father that he had been looking at maps again. He peered in and realized that it was Gump. He pushed the door open slightly, thinking to surprise him.

'But the thing is, Barti,' his uncle was saying, 'I just don't trust the man and I, of all people, should know. Remember that serving boy of his?' He paused and Bartolommeo grunted.

Blanco was just about to open his mouth to ask who when his uncle continued. 'And that cloak of his that matched his eyes? Who buys a cloak to match his eyes?'

Blanco paused. Gump was obviously talking about the Count. He pulled the door back towards him and placed his ear against the crack.

'What about his serving boy?' asked Bartolommeo. 'I don't remember him.'

'That's because he went missing,' replied Gump. 'Remember? One night he was there and the next morning he wasn't?'

'Probably ran away,' said Bartolommeo. 'Wouldn't be the first servant to run away from his master when he got the chance.'

Gump did not look convinced. 'That boy was terrified of him. I don't believe he would run away.'

'So what do you think happened?'

Gump leaned over the counter and whispered something in Bartolommeo's ear. Bartolommeo's eyes widened and then he gave a nervous laugh. 'No,' he said. 'Surely not.'

Blanco's curiosity finally became too much and he pushed open the door and marched in.

'What about his serving boy?' he asked.

Gump waved a hand merrily in the air. 'Nothing, nothing,' he said. 'Just a rumour, that's all. Have you come to map your journey?'

Blanco looked closely at his great-uncle but he was too upset about his father to pursue it any further at the moment.

'Papa says that I can't go,' he said. 'He says I have to stay and learn the business.'

Gump patted the seat next to him and motioned for Blanco to sit down. Bartolommeo had great chairs. They came from all over the world and one day the seat could be an elephant's head and the next a tiny carved stool from some mountain valley along the Silk Route. Today it was a monstrosity of a chair, towering over almost everything else in the shop and rising to a point. Blanco raised an eyebrow at Bartolommeo.

Bartolommeo wheezed and chuckled—he always wheezed because of all the dust from the maps. 'I swapped it for a map of Arabia,' he said. 'The man said it was from Kashmir and that it was a good omen to be pointing at the sky.'

Blanco sat down. It was incredibly uncomfortable.

'I think you should go,' said Gump.

'You said to think carefully earlier,' said Blanco.

'I've changed my mind,' said Gump. 'It'll do you good to get away.'

'But what about Papa?'

Gump harrumphed. 'You don't have to tell him,' he said. 'Just go! Do you think I asked my father before I went?'

Blanco stared at him. 'You went *with* your father,' he said.

'Exactly,' said Gump. 'But I didn't ask him first. He turned round and there I was. It was easier to take me with him than take me back.'

Blanco looked at Bartolommeo who was climbing

up a rickety old stepladder. All his maps were folded up so it was impossible to tell where they were for but he always seemed to know which one was which. His hand hovered over one for a moment and then he picked another one. Slowly he began to descend again.

'There's another thing,' said Gump.

'I thought there might be,' said Blanco.

'That Count has got something belonging to me.'

'A pickled quince?' ventured Blanco.

Blanco couldn't quite believe it but his uncle appeared to be blushing. Gump looked at Barti and then at Blanco. He leant over to him and whispered.

'You're tickling my ear,' said Blanco. 'And there's no one here except Bartolommeo. You don't have to whisper.'

Gump sighed. 'So much for secrets,' he said in disgust.

Blanco looked at him again. Yes, he was definitely blushing.

Gump took a deep breath, as though preparing for something unpleasant.

'The Count has some letters belonging to me,' he said eventually.

'Letters?' queried Blanco in disgust. He had been expecting a map leading to buried treasure at the very least. Letters!

'They're not just any letters,' replied his great-uncle crossly. 'They're very special letters.'

A horrible thought crossed Blanco's mind.

'They're not *love* letters, are they?'

Gump squirmed in his chair, looking awkward. 'They might be,' he said. 'They're my own private business.'

'No,' said Blanco, crossing his arms and settling himself as comfortably as he could in a very uncomfortable chair. 'I'm not getting anything for you unless you tell me the whole story.'

'Oh, very well,' said Gump crossly. 'Barti, you'd better pour some wine. It's a long story.'

The story that Gump had to tell started many years ago.

'It was just after I returned from my travels,' he began. 'Nobody would listen to a word I said. They all laughed at me or called me a liar. So I thought I'd go away for a while, just to get a rest from all the jeering. I wanted to go somewhere that I had never been before but not too far away. I had had enough of long journeys by that point. Eventually a friend suggested I tried the little island of Malta.'

Here Gump paused and took a sip of wine. His eyes grew soft and a little smile crossed his lips.

'I was bored there at first. After travelling so much it was hard to sit and do nothing. I walked the island. Every day I would get up and walk a little more and at night I would rest wherever I could. It was a lovely country . . . '

Blanco was growing impatient. 'But the letters,' he said. 'Hurry up and get to the letters.'

At first it seemed as though Gump hadn't heard him for he continued to extol the beauties of the Maltese countryside.

'And then one day,' he said eventually, 'I met this beautiful girl.' He stopped, lost in his memories, and didn't continue again until Barti nudged him in the ribs.

'She was called Magdalena,' said Gump, 'and she was the daughter of a local count. She wasn't meant to be out by herself but she had managed to escape her chaperone and was just wandering along the coast.' Gump sighed. 'She was so beautiful.'

Blanco and Barti raised eyebrows at each other. Neither had ever heard Gump talk about a woman like that before. Blanco wasn't sure how he felt about hearing about one now. After all, his uncle was in his sixties and he wasn't sure how happy his great-aunt would be about it all.

Gump shook himself. 'The letters are from her,' he said abruptly. And no matter how much Barti or Blanco encouraged him he would tell them nothing more about Magdalena or what had happened to her or why he had never mentioned her before.

'I'll tell you the rest if you bring the letters back,' he said finally.

'But what does the Count have to do with this?' asked Blanco. 'Why would he have taken your letters?'

Gump paused as though deciding the correct thing to say. 'He knew Magdalena too,' was all he said.

'Aha!' interrupted Blanco in the tone of one who thinks he is very clever because he has worked something out. 'So it's not because he knocked over your pickled quinces that you don't like the Count. It's because he's your love rival. Is that why you never mentioned before that you knew him?'

'Pah!' said Gump. 'What would you know about love. A tender sapling like you wouldn't have the first idea. Just get those letters for me and you might learn something about it.'

This stung Blanco. 'And what about Zia Donata?' he demanded. 'Does she know that you want me to find some old love letters for you?'

'You leave your great-aunt out of this,' said Gump abruptly. 'She knows all she needs to.'

'I have something for you, Blanco,' interrupted Barti, seeing that Marco was getting cross.

He waved a map at them and then spread it out across his desk. Blanco and Gump went over to look. It was a beautiful old map, full of drawings of strange and wonderful beasts. The forests, rivers, and mountains were marked out in remarkable detail. It was all drawn in a deep red ink which made it look as though it had been drawn in blood.

'Where is this for?' asked Blanco.

'It's a map to the Count's, of course,' said Barti.

'Why do you have a map pointing directly to the Count's castle?' asked Blanco suspiciously.

'Just do,' said Barti mysteriously. 'Someone must have sold it to me.'

Gump snorted in derision at Barti's mysterious manner. 'You mean the Count sold it to you?'

'Well, yes,' answered Barti. 'He practically gave it away, in fact. Insisted I took it.'

'Now that seems strange,' said Gump, 'almost as though he were leaving it here deliberately.' He chewed his lip and then turned to Blanco. 'I've decided. I don't think you should go, after all.'

Blanco heaved a great sigh of exasperation. 'First you say don't go, then you say go, now you say don't go again. Which is it to be? Why do you keep changing your mind?'

Gump made a face. 'I just don't trust the man. Remember, I've had dealings with him before. But I suppose you're a clever lad. You know how to keep out of trouble.'

'I'm going,' said Blanco. 'It's not your decision, it's mine. And I liked the Count. You just don't like him because of some rivalry you had with him in the past.'

Gump shrugged. Maybe he was biased. 'Well,' he said, 'if you're definitely going, will you get my letters back for me?'

Blanco shrugged. 'Well, I suppose since I'm going anyway, I may as well try.'

Count Maleficio looked into the mirror.

'Mirror, mirror on the wall . . .' he began and then he stopped. He rubbed it and slowly, very slowly, an image began to appear. It was of a tall, thin man with a pointed nose—not a large one, but a pointy one nonetheless. His eyes were silvery grey and shimmered like molten metal. They never stayed still for a second. He was dressed impeccably in silver grey; everything from the ruffled silk around his neck to his cloak was of the same colour as his eyes. His hair, too, was grey, beautifully coiffed and hanging to his shoulders. The Count tweaked a stray hair, made a few turns watching his cloak swirl in a satisfying way, and then smiled contentedly at his image in the mirror.

He turned to the table behind him. On it lay a bowl from which a vast amount of steam was rising. The Count blew on it gently and it turned a dark purple. He smiled again and rubbed his hands together, happy at what he saw. All around the room were dotted a multitude of machines, all in varying stages of completion.

As he looked into the bowl, the Count saw first of all his own reflection and then the room in which he was standing. As he continued to look the view changed to the outside of his room and he was gazing from outside his castle. He could see the tower where he was and if he looked very carefully he could see himself standing in one of the windows. Then his gaze turned away from the castle and went racing over the countryside. Eventually it reached Venice and it roamed around the streets for a while as though looking for something. After some time it settled on a shop in the via Margherita. As he watched the door opened and a boy came out. He looked scared and excited all at once.

'Come to me,' whispered the Count into the bowl. 'Come to me, Blanco.'

Chapter 3

For the rest of his life Blanco would always say that if only he had never set foot on the *Santa Maria* then his life would have turned out very differently. Even when he was a very old man he would sigh whenever anyone mentioned the name and sometimes it was hard to tell whether the sigh was of pleasure or pain.

The *Santa Maria* was a ship bound for Barcelona. The captain was a friend of Bartolommeo's and had agreed to let Blanco work his passage. Blanco soon discovered that Gump and Barti had everything all planned out for him. Gump must really want those letters back, thought Blanco. They had also filled a bundle full of useful things for him to take with him.

'Can't I say goodbye to Mama?' he asked.

'It would only put her in an awkward position with your father,' replied Gump. 'You know how she hates to keep secrets.'

Blanco thought ruefully of all the beatings that he had had from his father when his mother had accidentally given him away and nodded.

'I suppose it's for the best.'

Now, two days later, Blanco was wishing fervently for his mother. He had never felt so ill. Not even when he had had a wager with his friend Paolo to eat twenty spiced wafers as quickly as possible.

Blanco's time on the ship had not been quite as he had expected. As the cook's helper he was not supposed to appear above deck at all or allowed to speak to any of the passengers. When he had first entered the galley he had been sick almost immediately. The cook, looking at him in disgust—they had barely left port by this point—had sent him aloft to throw up over the side.

Blanco's last sight of Venice, therefore, was leaning over the side of the ship. Every so often, when his stomach relaxed slightly, he would look up to watch his home town recede into the distance. The captain had waited until the moon had risen and the canals had fallen silent. Then, like a spirit, the ship had slipped away from its mooring and out into the sea. The silhouettes of the palazzos rose like jagged teeth. Blanco felt a lump rise in his throat as he thought of his mother sitting at home, waiting for him to return. Was it too late to change his mind? Maybe running father's business wouldn't be all that bad. He thought of the sums and accounting he would have to do and then he thought of his flying machines and the Count's promise that together they would build a proper one and he knew he was right to go.

A small shape was walking along the harbour where their ship had been moored. Every so often it waved. Blanco blinked back the tears and waved back although he was fairly sure that he couldn't be seen. He knew that the figure was Gump come to wish him well.

It took weeks for Blanco's stomach to settle

enough for him to actually do some work for Alfredo the cook. Even then, he had to run up on deck with alarming frequency. It was on one such occasion, standing gazing out to sea, wondering how something so beautiful could play such havoc with his insides, that he heard the voice.

'Hello.'

Blanco turned round in surprise. He had thought he was alone on deck. He was confronted by a girl about the same age as himself. She was of Angelica's height and as fair as Angelica but that was where any similarity ended. Her hair looked not so much windswept as wind-scrubbed, standing out in an untidy tangle from her head. Her green eyes were large and bright but her nose was too small and her mouth too large for her face for her to be pretty. She was grinning happily at him.

'Hello,' replied Blanco, after first looking round to see if the captain was anywhere in sight.

'I'm Eva di Montini,' said the girl, holding out her hand.

'Blanco . . . ' replied he, and then hesitated, ' . . . Polo.' He did not want to use his father's name in case he were discovered.

The girl cocked her head to one side as though listening to something and then said, 'Are you related to the Signor Polo who travelled all the way to China?'

Blanco hesitated. If he admitted that he was then he might as well have used his proper name. But she looked so impressed that he found himself nodding.

'He's my great-uncle,' he said proudly.

Eva cocked her head again.

'Where is he now?' she asked.

'He's in Venice,' said Blanco, eyeing her movements suspiciously. When she cocked her head again, he asked, 'What are you doing? Are you listening for something?'

Eva grabbed his arm. 'You can't see them, can you? Oh, please say you can.'

'He can't see us, can he, Azaz?' asked Micha. She was standing against the mainsail and he had to squint to see her in the light. With her white robe she blended perfectly with the cloth behind her and only her bright blue eyes stared out, like two little pools of the sea that had been attached to the sail like brooches.

'No,' said Azaz. 'Look.'

Blanco was shaking his head and looking around Eva. He was staring at her as though she had been touched by the moon. Eva was gesticulating in the general area of the mainsail but Blanco still shook his head.

'This is going to be fun,' said Azaz from where he sat swinging his legs on the main beam. Anyone looking up may just have seen a flash of red, such as happens after looking into the sun for too long. 'I think this one has potential.'

Micha glanced up at him. 'Azaz,' she said. 'I think he may be the one.'

Azaz grinned down at her but before he could respond a tall thin woman appeared from the cabin areas and, catching sight of Eva and Blanco, marched towards them. 'Oh, oh,' said Azaz. 'Here comes trouble.'

'Oh no,' groaned Eva as the woman approached. She was tall and so thin that Blanco was virtually certain that if she stood behind one of the main ropes on deck she would be well nigh invisible. Her dress was of the same grey complexion as her skin. Her lips were pursed so tightly together they looked as though they begrudged every word that escaped from them. Her thin hair was scraped tightly back from her face, giving her a pained expression.

'Aunt Hildegard,' said Eva in a resigned tone as the said aunt came up and took her arm.

'Come away at once!' said Aunt Hildegard. 'I don't know why you can't stay below deck like a respectable young lady. And you certainly should not be speaking with one of the crew.'

Blanco was a touch aggrieved at that but knew better than to say anything.

'But, Aunt Hildegard,' began Eva, 'he is . . . '

'Hush!' cried her aunt as she fixed her claw-like fingers on to the upper part of Eva's arm. 'I don't wish to hear any more. And as for you, young man,' she turned her piercing blue eyes on him, 'you should know better than to talk to your betters. I shall complain to the captain.'

'Oh, please don't, Aunt Hildegard,' pleaded Eva. 'It was all my fault. I spoke to him first. He was only being polite in answering.'

Aunt Hildegard stared at them both and drew a long breath in through her thin nose. 'I suppose I could be persuaded to say nothing on this occasion. But if it should happen again I shall not hesitate to have you thrown off this ship.'

She turned on her heel and dragged a still protesting Eva away. Blanco laughed and then thought that he should probably go back downstairs to the galley. Alfredo would be wondering where he was. Just before he went, he hesitated. What had that girl said she had with her? Two angels? She had insisted that they were over by the mainsail. Blanco wandered over and grasped it. His hand caressed the rough linen weave of the cloth and then he gave a little laugh. He glanced up as a red flash of light caught his eye but before he could investigate any further the captain, catching sight of him, shouted at him to go below.

'Now you will sit there and do your sewing and there will be no more gallivanting about above deck,' said Aunt Hildegard crossly. She had only fallen asleep for the shortest time and had been most annoyed when she awoke and found that Eva had slipped out. She was not supposed to be left unchaperoned at any point. Aunt Hildegard was well aware of her duty to her brother's child.

Mutinously, Eva sat in the appointed chair and picked up her sewing. She grimaced at it. It was supposed to be a small embroidered wall-hanging but at the moment it resembled nothing so much as a rag that would be put to better use in cleaning the floor.

'Give me that,' said Aunt Hildegard, snatching it out of Eva's hands. She unwrinkled it and gazed at it in dismay. 'What have you done with it?'

'Nothing,' said Eva. 'Well, I've been sewing it, like you told me.'

'Sewing it?' cried Aunt Hildegard in disbelief. 'Most five year olds can sew better than this! And what have you done to make it so wrinkled? Slept on it?'

'Of course not!' cried Eva indignantly. No, what she had done was stamp on it a few times, roll it in a ball and kick it across the cabin but she saw no need to share this information with her aunt.

'What Señor Massana will say when you give him this, I shudder to think,' said Aunt Hildegard. 'He'll wonder how you've been brought up.' Her thin lips pursed even tighter together so that they disappeared completely. 'When I agreed to accompany you on this trip, your mother promised that you would be well behaved. And what do I find as soon as I turn my back but that you're off consorting with cabin boys!'

'He's not a cabin boy,' Eva snapped back. 'He's the cook's assistant.'

'Oh, well, that makes all the difference,' said her aunt nastily. 'That makes him perfectly respectable.'

'He is perfectly respectable,' said Eva. 'He's the great-nephew of Marco Polo.'

Aunt Hildegard snorted with disbelief. 'You have only his word for that! Did he offer you any proof?' When Eva shook her head, she snorted again. 'Respectable men do not work on ships,' she said sniffily.

Eva knew there was little point in saying more. Once Aunt Hildegard had made up her mind about someone that was it. She was so thoroughly respectable that Eva couldn't imagine her speaking to anyone to whom she hadn't been formally introduced about three times. She sighed and took her sewing back from her aunt. But although she said nothing more her mind was already buzzing with ideas of how to

meet up with Blanco Polo again. He was far too
interesting to be left alone.

'Pirates! Pirates dead ahead!'

Blanco could not control the frisson of fear and
excitement which shivered down his spine at the word
'pirates'. He rushed to the side and was rewarded
almost immediately by the sight of another ship bearing
down upon them at great speed. The pirate ship's hull
was formed from metal, constructed, he quickly
realized, in order to ram other ships and thus
immobilize them. Moreover, the ship flew no colours—
unlike the one on which Blanco was standing, which
flew the colours of the Venetian port—and its decks
were swarming with men. They were not only on the
deck but also up the main mast and hanging from the
sides. The amount of sea between Blanco's ship and
that great metal monster was shrinking rapidly. Blanco
stood stock still, torn between terror and fascination.

'What are you loitering about here for?' a crewman
shouted at Blanco. 'Get busy! Get in position, or, no,
get below deck and check the ladies are protected!
You're not likely to be of much use to us up here. I
doubt you've ever fought a battle in your life.'

Blanco was mildly offended at this slur upon his
ability to fight although he felt that this was not the
time to argue the point. Venice was not the most
peaceful place to have been brought up and a boy
learned to fight with his sword (and with his fists)
almost as soon as he could toddle. There were great
running fights through the *calli* in the summer time.

'Go on then!' shouted the crewman. Blanco was
given little choice as a sword was thrust in his hand,

he was pulled to the top of the stairs, and then practically pushed down them. He saved himself only by clutching at the thin rope that hung there, almost dropping his sword in the process.

Blanco had problems negotiating the stairs—the captain was swinging the ship around wildly in an attempt to stop the pirate ship from ramming them. Once down, he sped along the lower deck to the cabin where the passengers were and burst in to find Eva and her aunt there. Eva was obviously trying to get out of the cabin and was hampered by the fact that her aunt was hanging tightly onto her skirts and praying loudly to all the saints.

'Blanco!' cried Eva as she caught sight of him. 'Thank goodness someone has come to tell us what is going on! One of the crew just came and told us not to leave but wouldn't say why and I was just trying to go and find out when Aunt Hildegard detained me.' Her green eyes were wider than he had ever seen them and they had a frightened gleam.

Blanco thought that detained was a polite word, for Aunt Hildegard appeared to be gibbering with fear and was clutching on to Eva's ankles.

The boat lurched wildly and Blanco lost his balance and went swinging against the back wall, before managing to gasp out: 'It's pirates! We're under attack.'

Aunt Hildegard let out a shriek that could have raised blisters on skin and Blanco could only be grateful that they were on the opposite side of the ship from the side which the pirate ship was bearing down upon. The sight of that great metal beast plunging into them might have put paid to Aunt Hildegard for good.

Aunt Hildegard shrieked again at the shouts of the crewmen overhead and they heard the captain give the order to fire. Blanco wondered whether it would be enough. From what he had seen before being forced below stairs the pirate ship was bearing down upon them far too fast for many arrows to be fired.

Even though he was expecting it, the jolt that went through the ship as the pirate vessel struck stunned Blanco. It was as though his whole world had suddenly shifted sideways and he was thrown once again against the back wall. In the force of the attack Eva was thrown free from her aunt and she at once leapt to her feet and ran to the door of the cabin.

'Come on!' she said, turning to Blanco. 'I'm not staying down here waiting till they find us! Let's get out of here!'

Blanco jumped to his feet and started to run out after her, casting only a brief look at poor Aunt Hildegard who lay sprawled on the floor of the cabin, alternating between crying for Eva and calling on Holy Mother Mary to help her. He felt guilty at leaving her but this feeling was soon overcome by one of self-preservation as the sounds of the pirates boarding the ship filtered down the stairs. They might not hurt a harmless old woman but they might just run a sword through him . . . He ran but then stopped. He couldn't just leave her. Telling Eva to wait, he ran back into the cabin.

'Come with us!' he cried, trying to drag her to her feet.

She screamed louder. 'I can't!' she wailed. 'I'm too afraid!' Her fingers suddenly gripped his arms like talons and her eyes stared into his with an alarming intensity. 'Are you really related to Signor Marco Polo?'

'He is my great-uncle,' said Blanco, not really seeing why it was suddenly so important to her to check his lineage when they were under attack from pirates.

'Then I must ask you to take Eva! Save her!' she cried. 'Take her to her fiancé! Give me your word of honour!'

Blanco hesitated for the merest moment. Eva had managed to corner him every time he had raised his head above decks in the past few weeks and she was a very demanding companion. But Aunt Hildegard gave no sign of releasing him unless he did and so he gasped out an oath. She released her talon-like grip.

Blanco tried once more to make her get up but she would not move and cried: 'Go! Save yourselves!'

Reluctantly Blanco gave up and ran into the dimly lit passageway. Seeing Eva clutching a small package, he motioned for her to stay where she was and he darted down to his bunk in the galley and grabbed his bundle of belongings. Returning to where Eva stood he indicated that they should go up on deck. He crept slowly up the narrow stairs, Eva clutching determinedly to his hand as though she was scared that he would leave her behind too.

Blanco could not believe the sight that greeted him when he looked above deck. It was impossible to believe that one place could hold so many bodies, all heaving and swaying in what looked like a dance, albeit a deadly one. The captain was fighting like a dervish, his arms never stopping as they whirled about his body, striking at all within reach. As Blanco watched he struck down three pirates.

The pirate captain was not doing any fighting at that particular moment. He was clinging on to the rigging, directing his men all over the ship. He was an imposing figure, dressed entirely in black and with blood streaked across his face. One of the crew ran to attack him and the pirate ran him through with his sword without even pausing in his shouting. As he turned in their direction, Blanco could see that all his teeth were capped with gold.

And as for the noise! The great steel-works in Venice, the Arsenal, was quiet by comparison. Steel against steel, the thud of flesh hitting the ground or splashes as bodies hit the water. The shrieks of dying men and the triumphant cries of the pirates mingled together and were louder than any thunderclap. A hot, coppery tang of blood filled the air.

Despite the *Santa Maria*'s captain's prowess with his sword and his feet, his crew were fighting a losing battle. The pirates were like insects, swarming from their own ship on to this one. As soon as one was struck down another three appeared to take his place. To the watching Blanco's horrified fascination, the captain disappeared beneath a swarming mass of humanity and streams of blood began to flow towards the stairhead where they were standing. Blanco could not help thinking that they would be next.

'Do something, Azaz,' pleaded Micha.

They were floating above the ship, powerless to stop the mayhem below.

'What do you suggest?' snapped Azaz. 'That I go down and fight myself?'

'Of course not,' said Micha. 'But surely you can think of something.'

Azaz sighed and closed his eyes.

'I have an idea,' said Eva. She had stuck her head out beside Blanco's. 'Well, it's not exactly *my* idea but . . .'

'What?' demanded Blanco, his voice nearly giving away his fear by cracking. He struggled to bring it under control. 'Any suggestion would be good at this point.'

'I think we should make a run for it,' she said. 'If we slipped over the side furthest away from the pirates we could just swim to shore.'

Blanco didn't think that this was a good time to mention that he couldn't swim.

'Azaz says it will get dark in a minute,' Eva continued. 'That would be a good time to go, wouldn't it?'

'How do you know it will get dark?' asked Blanco suspiciously.

'Do you have another idea?' asked Eva and, to her credit, she did not sound sarcastic, merely curious.

'No,' said Blanco heavily, 'but—'

His 'but' was never fully uttered for at that moment something strange happened to the sun. Inch by inch its surface was covered by a dark shadow. It looked as though a giant beast were slowly chomping its way across it. At first the pirates and sailors were too busy fighting to notice but as the darkness increased it became impossible to ignore. Some fell to their knees. Some cried out for mercy but some carried on killing regardless of any evil omens.

Blanco did not stop to see what would happen next. Grabbing Eva's hand he raced across the deck and they jumped into the sea, calling on St Nicholas for assistance as they did so. He sank instantly but with one hand he kept a tight grip of Eva and the other he held as high as possible in order to keep his belongings, and especially his map, dry. After kicking his feet vigorously for a moment, his head broke through the surface again, Eva beside him. Half the sun had now disappeared, which worried Blanco, but not as much as the thought of his head going back under water. Something nudged his back and it was with a sigh of relief that he turned to find a large plank of wood. He made Eva climb on to it and then he held on to the other end and kicked for where he thought the shore was. He might not know how to swim but he was fairly certain that kicking your legs had something to do with it. It was getting darker all the time and Blanco was uneasy.

'I don't like this darkness,' he said.

Eva was lying on her front on the wood and paddling with her hands. 'It's perfectly natural,' she replied, sounding not in the least bit worried. 'The sun will come back soon. Azaz says so. He says a shadow has fallen over the sun but that soon it will pass.'

Blanco did not feel happy with this answer—who was Azaz again?—but he knew there was nothing he could do about it. With a sigh he kicked his legs with greater determination and headed for what he hoped was land.

'Well done, Azaz,' said Micha. 'An inspired move, starting the eclipse.'

Azaz gave a nonchalant shrug. 'I knew those fools on the ship would be terrified by it.' He paused and looked at where the sun was still clothed in darkness. 'I suppose it is quite frightening if you don't know what it is.'

'We know the light will return,' said Micha. 'They don't.'

'Dammit all,' said the Count, looking in his bowl. He could see the vast open sea and the tiny wooden plank on which Eva and Blanco were riding. 'That wasn't meant to happen. The girl was meant to die with the rest.'

He called for Griffin and when Griffin arrived, he kicked him.

Chapter 4

—❖—❖—

'Holy Mother, full of grace . . . '

Blanco was reeling off his prayers in gratitude on his knees while Eva wandered around the forest in which they found themselves. He had never been so terrified as he was when clinging on to that plank and praying that they would reach land and now that they had he was making his gratitude known. The sun had stayed dark for some time and then eventually it had reappeared, this time looking as though a great beast was spitting it out piece by piece. By the time it was fully light again both the ships had disappeared and they were floating alone in the middle of the sea. Blanco had been worried until he looked behind him and saw land.

'Blanco,' cried Eva. 'Look at this!'

And that was another thing, thought Blanco. What was he supposed to do with Eva? He had promised her aunt that he would look after her but that promise had been made under duress. Surely no one would blame him if he reneged on it now and dropped her off at the nearest convent? He had to get to the Count's castle as quickly as possible. What if the Count made a successful flying machine without him? What if he actually *flew* without him? He didn't have time for detours. He looked round at his belongings which lay strewn around him drying in the sun. Despite his best efforts his bundle had suffered a quick dipping in the sea and most things were wet. Thankfully the map had been protected by the leather case he kept it in.

'Blanco!' she called again and he slowly got to his feet.

'Look!' she cried. 'It's a church!'

Blanco looked in the direction she was pointing and saw the spire of what seemed indeed to be a church.

'Come on then,' he said resignedly, gathering up his things. 'Let's find out where we are.'

'Do you know what's going to happen next, Micha?' asked Azaz.

Micha shook her beautiful golden head but she was smiling. She was glad that Blanco had to look after Eva.

'I do,' said Azaz and he laughed.

'Where is your fiancé?' asked Blanco crossly as they walked towards the church. He knew it wasn't Eva's fault (although a small part of him felt unreasonably that maybe it was) but that didn't stop him feeling annoyed at having to chaperone her.

'Barcelona,' replied Eva happily. 'But don't worry. I'll just go wherever you're going.' She was delighted to be off the ship and was gathering up flowers as they went along. Her clothes were drying nicely in the sun, she had got rid of Aunt Hildegard, and she didn't have to get married any more.

'No, you will not,' replied Blanco, heaving a sigh of relief. Barcelona wasn't that far out of his way. 'I promised to deliver you to your fiancé and that's where I'll take you. Unless I can find someone else going that way.' He muttered the last quietly under his breath and if Eva heard him she gave no sign of it.

'His name is Señor Massana,' continued Eva, 'and he's old enough to be my grandfather. I think it would be very mean of you to take me there.'

'I don't have time to take you back to Venice,' said Blanco. He ignored the part about her fiancé being old enough to be her grandfather. He didn't want to get into a discussion about that.

'I don't want to go back there either,' she said cheerily. 'They'd only send me away again.' She paused. 'They're only doing it because of my angels, you know.'

Blanco stopped, looking annoyed. 'Look,' he said. 'We've both just had a terrible scare. But there's no need to talk about angels again.'

'But I told you about them before,' said Eva. 'Azaz was the one who made the sun dark and told us to jump off the ship.'

'I thought you said he was the bad one,' said Blanco.

'I knew I'd told you about them,' said Eva complacently. 'And he's not bad as such, just a bit mischievous. He likes you.'

Blanco shook his head. He wasn't surprised that her family was sending her away if she continually talked about angels. He knew that holy women could sometimes hear voices from heaven but he found it hard to imagine anyone less like a holy woman than Eva.

'Here we are,' he said cheerily, determined to change the subject. He tried to push open the door of the church. It was stiff and heavy so Blanco gave it a hefty shove and it flew open.

Immediately their ears were assailed by a loud wailing. The sound was so miserable and so distraught that Blanco and Eva stared at each other hesitantly, neither of them being very enthusiastic about entering the church now. Then Blanco squared his shoulders. It was his responsibility to look after Eva and therefore it was his responsibility to find out where they were. He motioned to Eva to stay where she was and moved into the church.

There was a party of four standing at the altar—three men and one wailing woman. They were obviously pilgrims for they were dressed in long heavy robes, wore wide-brimmed hats, and each of them had a number of tokens pinned to their cloaks to show which shrines they had visited.

Blanco was still staring at them and wondering how one little woman could make so much noise when Eva nudged him from behind.

'I thought I told you to stay outside,' he whispered ferociously.

Eva ignored his tone. 'How,' she said in her usual clarion tones, 'can one woman make so much noise?'

It was unfortunate that at that very moment the wailing stopped and Eva's question fell into the silence that followed.

'My name is Clara,' said the once-wailing woman in an apologetic manner, coming towards them. 'I always cry when I get near holy sites.'

Her companions nodded vigorously in agreement.

'We have been praying at the shrine,' the woman

continued. 'But we can always make room for more if you wish to pray also.'

'Oh no,' said Blanco hastily. 'We haven't come here to pray. We're lost.'

'But if you have lost your way,' said one of the men from behind Clara, 'then surely prayer is the best direction.'

'We're not spiritually lost,' interrupted Eva. 'We're *really* lost. Our ship was attacked by pirates and we had to swim to shore and now we have no idea where we are!'

This explanation was met by a bemused silence.

'It's true,' said Blanco. 'If you could just show us on our map where we are and the correct direction in which to head then we can leave you in peace.'

He had taken Bartolommeo's map out of his bag and laid it on the ground as he spoke. One of the male pilgrims came over to look.

'Gunther,' he said, introducing himself. 'What a beautiful map.'

The other pilgrims came round to look and to offer advice. It quickly became clear that Clara was the leader of the group.

'Now look,' she said, pointing to a spot just before the high mountains of the Pyrenees. 'This is where we are now. This village is too small to be marked on your map but it is just about here. Now where do you want to go?'

'Here,' said Blanco, pointing to Barcelona.

'Here,' said Eva, pointing to the mark that Blanco had made to show Count Maleficio's castle. Blanco scowled at her.

Clara looked at them both shrewdly and then smiled. 'You have to go past here,' she put her finger on the mark for the Count's castle, 'to get to Barcelona,' she said. 'And whichever your destination, you have to first cross over the Pyrenees. We,' and she indicated her three fellow pilgrims, 'are headed for the great pilgrim site at Santiago de Compostela which also lies on the other side of the Pyrenees. Why don't you travel with us until then? It is always safer to travel in a larger party than a smaller one.'

Blanco thought that this was an excellent idea and was just about to say so when Eva beat him to it. 'We'd love to,' she said and the matter was decided.

Eva was happier than she had been in a long time. Wandering along the road with an unusual group of people in a strange land seemed to her to be the epitome of happiness. No more father telling her not to talk to anyone, no more mother tutting at her, and no more sister making horrible remarks. This, she thought, was freedom.

'When did you first hear them, my dear?' asked Clara.

That was another joy. Clara, who wailed when within sight of saints, thought that it was perfectly normal for Eva to have two angels who followed her around.

'A few years ago,' replied Eva, 'when I was about ten. I'm not sure who was the more surprised. I was sitting in the church, saying my penance, and I heard these two voices. I was sure I was the only one in the church and when I shouted out they stopped talking. But then they started again.'

'What were they talking about?' asked Clara.

'Something about how cold the church was,' said

Eva. 'Nothing particularly exciting. I did ask them how many of them could dance on the head of a pin but they just laughed at me and said that they were bigger than any human and since no human could dance on the head of a pin, what chance had they?'

'Are they here now?' asked Clara. 'Are they listening to us?'

'I don't think so,' said Eva. 'They're not with me all the time. Sometimes they go off and do . . . ' she paused and then shrugged, ' . . . angel things. I don't know why they stay with me, really. Mostly they try to keep me out of trouble.'

'Do they manage?' asked Clara with a twinkle in her eye. She had a feeling that Eva could be quite a handful when she put her mind to it.

Eva laughed. 'Sometimes they get me into more of it. Usually when I get caught talking to them.' She sobered. 'That's why I'm being sent away to marry a man old enough to be my grandfather. They're hoping that he won't have heard tales of me talking to them.'

'And how did you meet Blanco?' asked Clara, trying to take Eva's mind off the subject.

Eva looked at Blanco, who was walking just ahead of them, with adoring eyes. She had never met anyone like him before.

'He saved me from Aunt Hildegard and from pirates,' she said. 'Isn't he wonderful?'

Blanco, who had been listening in to the conversation, jumped in horror and started talking loudly to Gunther about fighting.

Micha looked at Blanco and Eva and smiled. It was all coming together nicely. She had arranged for Eva to talk to Blanco on the ship and for Aunt Hildegard to make sure that Blanco took on the responsibility for Eva. It was amazing what a word or a thought in the right ear could do.

Micha hovered above the group, her long white robes flowing about her, her golden wings quivering with the effort of holding her there. The warmth of the sun caressed the golden feathers like a gentle breeze, causing them to shine brightly. Micha loved her wings and was glad that they had been returned to her after her fall. She had never felt right without them. But then the sacrifice had been worth it, even though she now had a constant pain in her heart from having them put back on.

She smiled down at Eva. She was happy to see her chattering away and looking so cheerful. She would make sure that Eva did not make the same mistake that she had.

Griffin stared at the blocks of wood and the pile of feathers. He sneezed. He wandered over to the window and stared out. He felt a little dizzy. He was in the top floor of the tower of a castle, perched high on a cliff. Looking out, Griffin felt that he could see the whole world although, in reality, he couldn't even see the next village.

The Count had asked him to prepare the

potion. Griffin hated preparing the potion. But if he didn't do it the Count might just throw him out of the window. He had threatened to do so often enough. He rubbed his eyes, feeling again the stubbly patches where his eyebrows used to be. He felt his forehead, missing the feel that his fringe used to make.

He sighed and turned away from the window towards the mirror. 'Come on, fly boy,' he said. 'Hurry up and get here.'

'So you see,' said Blanco. 'What I want to do more than anything in the world is to build a flying machine. And now the Count has invited me. Only I have to take care of Eva. And I was wondering, if you were going to Barcelona, then maybe . . . '

Here his voice petered out as he looked guiltily back at where Eva was walking along with Clara.

He was walking with the other pilgrims. They had told him that they were seeking the shrine of the Blessed Ignato which lay just inside French territory, on the border with Spain. Ignato was famous for the form of his martyrdom (torn apart by a pack of wild dogs) and was also reputed to be able to cure those who suffered from an excess of wind.

From what the pilgrims had said Ignato had had a terrible life. He had been hounded from town to town, had been stoned twice and miraculously saved both times, once by a marvellous hailstorm where the hail was reputedly larger than the stones which the crowd were raining down on him. The second time he escaped because so few of the stones hit him and he managed to run away before the crowd picked them all up again. Blanco had argued that the second time wasn't particularly miraculous—maybe the crowd were just bad shots—but Clara insisted that that may be so but it was God who had made them bad shots in the first place. She said that she knew that Ignato had a very miserable existence because she was already feeling a little bit sniffly, even though they were still a long way from the shrine.

The pilgrims were laden down with mementos from each shrine that they had visited: candles and feathers and badges and tiny wax replicas. None of them had ever visited a major shrine before but that was where they were heading now.

Blanco was walking with Clara's husband, Bolbo, and the other two pilgrims, Gunther and Cosimo. He grimaced in sympathy when Bolbo explained that the wailing had been going on for over five years.

'She can't help it,' he said in a mild, uncomplaining voice.

'No, she can't help it,' chimed in Gunther, who was walking on the other side of Blanco, in a voice which clearly said that he wished she could.

Gunther came from Bavaria and had met up with Clara and Bolbo when they passed through his village. He was a wood carver by trade and had decided that he could carve wood quite as well walking as sitting. Besides, all the girls in his village were married and he had decided that if he wanted a wife he would have to make an effort to find one. He was carving a piece of wood as he walked. It was an uncanny likeness of a wolf that he said he would be able to sell to somebody who lived in or near a forest.

'They'll put it above their door,' he explained. 'So

that any wolves that are prowling about will know that their house is under the protection of the Great Wolf.'

Bolbo crossed himself at that and muttered something about hanging a cross above the door instead but Gunther just laughed and said that many of the peasants where he came from trusted more in nature and the old beliefs than Christ. He finished his carving and gave it to Blanco.

Nobody, including Cosimo, knew where he was from but he had joined up with Clara, Bolbo, and Gunther somewhere near Toulouse.

Blanco had been glad to meet up with these new companions. Not only because it was good to have company—and the greater safety of a larger party— but also because they were a possible means of getting rid of Eva. Blanco was even now trying to find out if they planned to go to Barcelona after their visit to the shrine at Santiago de Compostela. He knew that they did not plan to go home after visiting there, but intended to continue travelling and visit yet more pilgrim sites and he hoped that Barcelona would be on their route.

'No,' said Micha.

'No,' said Azaz.

'They must stay together,' said Micha.

'I want to see him fly,' said Azaz. 'I want to see if these humans can do it.'

'Not like we can,' said Micha, lying on her back and floating along, riding the wind currents, her body undulating to their movements.

'No,' said Azaz, walking along beside her. He didn't like to fly much any more. 'They will be clumsy. But I want to see it. And I want to see what else he and that Count will make together. I think their minds will merge well. They have a perfect alchemy.'

'I want Eva to stay with him,' said Micha, looking forlorn. 'I want her to be happy. He can't leave her behind.' She stood up, looking determined. 'He won't leave her behind.'

'Be careful, Micha,' warned Azaz. 'You know what happened last time.'

'Blanco!' cried Eva running up to grab his arm. 'Are you planning to leave me?'

Blanco looked at her, a little unsure of how to respond. He was trying to leave her, of course, but he felt unaccountably guilty about it. He shook his head, trying to dislodge the guilt. He barely knew the girl. But the promise he had made to her Aunt Hildegard kept echoing in his ears. She looked so forlorn as she stared at him that he felt even worse.

'No,' he eventually sighed. 'No. I'll take you to Barcelona.'

'See,' whispered Eva fiercely to herself. 'I told you he wouldn't leave me, Azaz.'

The Count stared again at the chart. It was a mass of lines, dots, and squiggles. He traced one particular line with his finger. The nail was long and pointed and left a faint trace of its route. At the start and end of the line were two large crosses.

'Look at this, Griffin,' called Count Maleficio.

Griffin shuffled over. His leg still hurt him where the Count had kicked him the day before. He rubbed his eyes. They were itchy along the line of his eyelid, prickly as the hair slowly grew back in.

'Do you know what this means?' asked the Count, pointing out the line.

Griffin looked at the beautifully drawn chart. He searched through his befuddled brain, trying to remember what the Count had said last time. He was asked this question often but his poor brain retained little information. That was why the Count liked him but it also infuriated him on occasion.

'That's your saviour,' he cried out at last in a rush of remembrance, pointing to the first cross. 'And that's . . . ' His hand hovered over the second cross. His finger momentarily touched it, leaving a large smudge. He flinched away from the Count and hastily finished, ' . . . that's your neme—neme—' He struggled over the word.

'My nemesis, you dolt!' cried the Count, cuffing him, infuriated at the large smudge on his impeccably drawn astrological chart. 'My saviour and my nemesis!'

He looked at the chart once more, cursed loudly, and then turned to look into the bowl. The smoke it was billowing today was blue. The boy now had a whole collection of people with him. Good, maybe they would take the *girl. When he squinted he could see lights around her head. Lights were never good. They tended to interfere with his work. He looked again. They were at a river. He felt his excitement rising. He was nearly here.*

Chapter 5

'You cannot cross unless you pays me!' the boatman was shouting.

'But we are pilgrims,' replied Bolbo. 'We have little money and it would be a good thing that you would do if you would take us across.'

'Pilgrims! Pah!' And he suited the action to his words by spitting on the ground in front of them. 'You pilgrims are nothing but a nuisance to those of us who live here. All the food prices are put up during pilgrim season and our roads get congested and it becomes impossible to even get to the next village! And you expect to get everything for free or for a blessing. I say you pays or you doesn't go!'

He was quite adamant about it. There were quite a number of boatmen along the bank but none were offering to take the group. There was obviously some kind of rota system in operation. Indeed, as Blanco's group watched, another group of pilgrims reached the riverside and one of the remaining boatmen approached them and started the same type of conversation.

'I wonder if there is a bridge or another boatman in the area,' murmured Clara. 'I don't think I'd like to cross with this man. By the sounds of it, he would like to see us all drowned.'

Bolbo was studying the pilgrim's guidebook.

'What does it say?' asked Blanco.

'*Don't pay the ferryman*,' Bolbo replied. 'There are no bridges marked at all and the other boatmen on this stretch seem to be just as churlish as this fellow,' he continued. 'I wonder if we could wade across.'

The group eyed the river at his words. It was a possibility for it was not too wide but it did appear to be very fast flowing in the middle, fast enough to sweep the lighter members of the party off their feet. It was not such a possibility as it first appeared.

'Does the book suggest any other way to cross the river?' asked Clara.

'No,' replied Bolbo.

'How much are you asking, fellow?' Gunther asked the boatman.

He grinned maliciously and named his price.

Blanco was not alone in spluttering at the amount which was ridiculously high. Blanco felt that the boatman might as well have hit them all over the head and just demanded the money.

Blanco was particularly put out for he would have to pay for Eva as well, for when they had leapt overboard from the ship after the pirates attacked they had each clutched in their hands a small bag. Blanco's contained Barti's map and a bag of coins. Eva's had contained only clothes, for her Aunt Hildegard had had control of all the money they had.

'Maybe some of us could swim it to save money?' Eva suggested brightly. Blanco shivered, remembering again the sensation of his head under water after jumping off the ship. Eva seemed to have an unhealthy regard for water!

'No swimming here,' came the reply of the

boatman. 'If you start to swim we clubs you over the head and then you don't swim much further.' He grinned widely and made drowning motions with his hands.

The men were clearly criminals, using the boat trip to furnish their own pockets. But it also appeared that the group had little choice but to pay him. They had to cross this river to reach the Pyrenees which they could clearly see in front of them.

Grumbling and muttering they all paid their dues and then the males of the party drew back to let the females all get into the boat and be ferried across first.

'All in!' cried the boatman, quite cheerful now that he had a pocket full of coins.

'But there quite clearly is not enough room for us all!' cried Clara, her hands going to her face in fear. 'The boat will overturn.'

'All in,' repeated the boatman firmly. 'Or nones of you comes in.'

'Look,' pointed Bolbo. 'The other group have all got in that boat and it seems to be holding.'

The other group who had reached the river round about the same time as them had indeed got into another boat. They were about the same number and although they looked uncomfortably cramped the boat did seem to be steady. Boat was a kind word to use. They were little more than hollowed out tree trunks. The bark was still on this one and, on closer inspection, Blanco could see that there were little branches still attached.

There seemed to be nothing else for it but to climb in. Gunther handed the ladies in first and then

Blanco and Bolbo clambered in and squashed in where they could. The boat rocked precariously but stayed firm in the water.

'At least it's not too far across the river,' murmured Clara, trembling. She had admitted to Eva that she had a terrible fear of water.

Blanco looked downriver at the other boat which was just a little ahead of theirs. They were now in the fastest flowing part of the river and as he watched he saw their boatman start to rock the boat wildly and some of the pilgrims on board stood up to protest. Of course, as soon as they stood up the boat became even more unbalanced and, in front of his horrified eyes, tipped over, ridding itself of all, except the boatman who had somehow managed not only to stay in the boat but also to keep it upright.

Blanco was not the only one to see the upset party for Gunther and Cosimo were also facing that way and they all cried out at the sight.

'Stay calm,' said Gunther, managing to make everyone stay in their seats even as some of the party tried to rise. 'Stay calm or you'll set us off too. Look, some of the other boats are going to their rescue.'

Sure enough, the boatmen who did not have passengers had set off from the riverbank in pursuit of the distressed pilgrims, most of whom were struggling in the water. When they reached the first couple of pilgrims they leaned over in order, Blanco thought, to pull them in but instead he saw, to his horror, that they were stealing from them, pulling rings off fingers and bags off backs and then flinging the pilgrims back in the water to struggle ashore as best they might while they rowed back to the bank.

'Thieves!' he shouted jumping to his feet, despite

Gunther's attempt to stop him. 'Murdering, vile thieves!'

'Shut up!' growled the boatman. 'Or I'll do the same with you lot. Just be grateful I've got to be home early today or I would have done it anyway.'

'But how can you be so blatant about such deliberate cruelty?' asked Clara. 'You obviously do this often. Have none complained?'

'Who's there to complain to?' asked the boatman, completely unconcerned. 'There ain't no one out here between us and the other side of them mountains and once you're across the river you're hardly going to come back over this side. Leastways not without getting in a boat you're not. And who's going to want to do that once they've had a dunking?'

'How many people have been killed?' asked Bolbo with horror in his voice.

'Oh, we rarely kills anyone,' said the boatman cheerily. 'Most make it to the other side. Just without their possessions.'

'But these are pilgrims you are doing this to,' said Clara. 'These people are on a holy mission. They have been blessed by the church. What you are doing is a sin, a grievous sin.'

'Yes,' he replied grinning. 'But we repents often. And it's not like we asked you all to come this way.'

His sheer audacity struck them all into silence, particularly since they were in the fastest flowing part of the river themselves now and none of them wanted to end up in the water.

They sat in mute silence watching their fellow-pilgrims stagger on to the shore further downriver. Blanco counted them all and saw that they had indeed all made it. The boats had headed back to the opposite shore now and they could hear a lot of yelling and jeering from them.

The boatman had ferried the boat almost the full way across the river when Cosimo pointed out that there was no landing stage at the other side.

'Where do you land your boat?' Clara asked the boatman.

'Well, I stops it here,' he answered amiably, 'and you all get off.'

'But . . . but, we're not on land yet,' said Eva.

'No, but this is as close as I take you,' he said. 'I would recommend that you steps out of the boat now and you'll just get your feet wet. Otherwise I shall tip the boat and you'll get more than your feet wet.'

'You really are a most scurrilous criminal,' said Clara as they all stepped out of the boat into the water.

It wasn't cold but it was definitely wet and it is never particularly pleasant to have water squelching about at the bottom of one's boots.

'I shall complain of you at the first town we reach,' Clara continued.

'Complain away,' answered the boatman beginning to row himself back to the far shore. 'They won't do nothing about it. Have a good trip now!'

And with a cheery wave of his hand he was off leaving the group fuming on the river bank.

'Yeuch! Soggy feet!' Blanco said in disgust, lifting one wet-booted foot off the ground and shaking it and then the other.

'You should have taken them off like Micha suggested,' stated Eva, as she dried her feet on the grass and then placed them back inside her dry boots.

'Some of us didn't have the chance,' Blanco muttered grimly, for the men had been made to leave the boat first—the boatman obviously had some small iota of chivalry within his miserable criminal body.

'At least we have all our belongings,' said Clara. 'Unlike the poor party who were thrown into the river and then stripped of all they possessed. I think that we should take up a collection for them.'

Azaz was tempted for a moment to do something to the boatmen to make them pay for what they had done but he restrained the urge. It was interfering in other people's destinies that had got him into trouble in the first place. He contented himself with causing one large wave to crash over the boat, soaking the boatman and wiping the grin from his face.

Azaz strode along behind the group of pilgrims, his wings tucked in tidily down his back, his long red robes flapping around his ankles, his ruby belt gleaming like the berries on a holly tree. Unlike Micha, he didn't like to use his wings unless he had to. They reminded him too much of what he had lost.

His gaze fell on Blanco. The boy's mind interested him in a way that reminded him of why he had chosen to fall. Insatiable curiosity, the need to try out new things, an enthusiasm for new technologies—these were all things that Azaz had wanted to teach and share but he had had to make a sacrifice to do so. He had to be careful not to say too much this time, not to interfere.

He was trying to atone for past mistakes after all, not make new ones.

Eva couldn't sleep. She tossed one way and then turned to the other side but nothing seemed to work. Everywhere she turned she felt uncomfortable. But it was more than that. Her mind was continually wandering, darting from one thought to another in quick succession. She couldn't pin any of them down as they flitted through her consciousness and she grew tired of chasing them.

She gave up, opened her eyes, and looked over at her fellow companions. The pilgrims were all curled up tightly in their cloaks and were sleeping the sleep of those whose souls were safe. She glanced over at Blanco who lay on her other side but he also appeared to be sleeping soundly. She gave herself up to her thoughts.

The day that her mother had taken her aside and told her of the plans that her father had for her had been the worst day of her life. She had never wanted to leave Venice, had been horrified when she heard that her strict Aunt Hildegard was to accompany her, and devastated when she heard that the man she was to marry was older than her own father. Stepping on to the ship she thought that she had said goodbye to all her dreams for she could see no chance for escape, not with Aunt Hildegard seemingly attached to her side. But then she had met Blanco and everything had changed. He was a strange boy, with his dreams of flying. She knew he didn't really want her along on his journey but she also knew that he wouldn't desert her.

The object of her thoughts turned over at that moment and she reached over and tapped him lightly on his shoulder.

'Blanco,' whispered Eva. 'Are you awake?'

'No,' replied Blanco screwing his eyes shut tighter and shrugging her hand off. 'I'm fast asleep and dreaming that I am travelling alone.'

'Oh,' said Eva, sitting back on her heels. 'I was sure you were awake.'

Blanco sighed and rolled on to his back. He opened his eyes. Above him was the sky and the stars glittering on it. It looked as if a painter had flicked his silver paint across a dark canvas. Blanco gazed at them for a moment longer and then turned to look at Eva. She was kneeling beside him, her eyes wide with anxiety.

'What is it?' he asked.

'Why do you want to fly?' she asked.

Blanco looked at her incredulously. 'You've woken me up to ask me that?' he asked. 'Couldn't you have waited till morning?'

Eva bit her lip. 'I couldn't sleep,' she said.

Blanco wasn't surprised at this. Most nights the group slept in a hostel but sometimes, like tonight, they found no dwelling places as night fell and they had to camp out. They built a fire and slept round it in their thick pilgrims' cloaks. Blanco enjoyed sleeping under the stars but he didn't enjoy the hard ground with its little bits of twigs and stones and who knew what else which dug into him, no matter how carefully he cleared the ground before laying his cloak down. It had taken him a long time to fall asleep this time and he was not happy about being woken.

'I just do,' he said grumpily. 'I've always wanted to.'

'But do you really have to go and visit this Count?' Eva persisted. 'Can't you build one yourself?'

'No,' said Blanco, getting enthused despite his tiredness. 'No, you see, the Count has a proper workroom, with lots of materials with which to experiment. And he lives in a castle on a cliff with a very very high tower.' Here he paused for effect.

'Why does that matter?' asked Eva.

'It gives more chance of flying,' said Blanco. 'If you can catch the wind currents you could fly for a long time.'

'Or you could get killed,' said Eva.

'We have a tower on our palazzo at home,' continued Blanco dreamily. 'That was where I first tried to fly. It's not high enough though. I think that—'

'Blanco, I think the Count may be a bad man.'

Blanco stopped his musings and looked up at the sky.

'Look at the stars, Eva,' he said, with happiness in his voice. 'Look at how far away they are, how beautiful, how free.'

Eva lay down beside him and silently stared up into the sky. It was true—they were beautiful.

'Imagine being up there,' sighed Blanco. 'Imagine floating with the stars. I wonder what they look like close up.'

'My mother used to say that they were the fires of all those who had died,' said Eva dreamily. 'She said that if you whistled they would come a little closer. Not that she ever encouraged me to whistle,' she added hastily. 'That would have been unladylike. And not that she didn't believe in heaven either.'

Blanco was interested in what Eva had to say. This was the first time that she had voluntarily mentioned her mother. But first he pursed his lips and tried a gentle whistle. He didn't want to be too loud in case he woke the pilgrims.

'Eva,' he cried in delight. 'It works.'

'Of course it works,' said Eva. 'My mother is never wrong.'

Blanco looked at her and was about to ask her something about her family but before he could do so they both heard something else in the darkness.

'What was that?' Eva asked in a terrified voice.

It came again and one by one the hairs on the backs of their necks began to rise.

It was a wolf; and it sounded hungry and very, very close.

They could see from where they lay that it appeared to be injured. Neither of them moved. The pilgrims continued to sleep, Cosimo even going so far as to give a little snore and turn over. Eva's eyes were stretched so wide that Blanco wouldn't have been surprised if they had fallen out.

Blanco was fairly sure that he knew what the wolf had his eye on. The pieces of dried meat in his satchel were an obvious enticement.

The wolf snarled again and started towards them, dragging its injured paw behind it. It obviously saw the sleeping pilgrims as prey and who could blame it—even with its injured paw it could outrun all of them, and then that large jaw, those sharp teeth . . .

Its yellow eyes glittered ominously in the darkness. Blanco shivered and looked again at Eva who was still in the same position, eyes wide, mouth open.

Blanco slipped from his cloak, towards his satchel. Maybe if he threw it further away the wolf would go after it and leave them all alone. He had just got his hand on it when he saw, out of the corner of his eye, the wolf preparing to leap. And he wasn't leaping for the satchel but instead leapt straight at Eva. She was less of a challenge, lying prostrate on the ground. Blanco's hand curled around something in his satchel. He pulled it out and threw it at the wolf. It was the carving of a wolf that Gunther had given him and its sharp edges drew blood as it struck the real wolf on the nose. It howled in anguish but it stopped long enough for Blanco to know what to do next.

He leapt for the fire, grabbed one of the burning branches, and thrust it straight into the wolf's face. It stopped in mid-leap as it howled again in agony and fell in an untidy heap. Blanco and Eva could smell the singed hairs from its face and could see the burn when the wolf gave them a malevolent glare from the far side of the fire.

Blanco brandished the fiery branch at it again and it slunk backwards beyond the rim of their vision.

'What's going on?' asked Gunther, roused from sleep and instantly on his feet.

'It was a wolf!' said Blanco, still breathing heavily.

The other pilgrims had woken at the noise too and, horrified, Clara comforted the now weeping Eva. She could not quite believe the close escape that she had had. If Blanco had not been so quick. She shivered and Clara hugged her. It just didn't bear thinking about.

It took a long time for anyone to fall asleep again. Blanco didn't. Throughout the night, for he did not dare sleep, he heard periodic growls but the wolf never approached them again.

That night the Count smashed up his tower room and Griffin cowered in the corner.

Chapter 6

It was time to say goodbye to the pilgrims. Since the night of the wolf attack, their journey had progressed smoothly. Together they had travelled over the mountains. Together they had marvelled at the sight from the top and together they had made their way down, into the land of Spain. Clara had told them stories of the saints, Gunther had sung them songs from his homeland, and Bolbo and Cosimo had entertained them too. But now it was time to part for the pilgrims had to turn right to get to Santiago de Compostela and Blanco and Eva had to turn left for the Count's castle and Barcelona.

'Goodbye, darling Clara,' said Eva, giving her a hug. 'I hope you enjoy Santiago. And if you ever find yourself in Barcelona please, please come and look me up. I'll be in Señor Massana's house.' Here Eva cast a pleading look at Blanco but he either didn't see it or he ignored it as he was too busy saying his farewells to Bolbo, Gunther, and Cosimo.

'You'll be fine,' said Clara, stroking Eva's perennially untidy hair. 'Blanco's a good boy. He'll do the right thing.'

'For him or for me?' asked Eva.

Clara smiled. 'For both of you,' she said, leaving Eva strangely comforted.

Blanco and Eva waved until the pilgrims were out

of sight. Then they turned and looked at the dusty road ahead of them. Without saying a word to each other they started walking. Both had plenty to think about.

Eva was preoccupied with thoughts of Señor Massana and Barcelona and, most of all, with thoughts of how to persuade Blanco not to take her there. Azaz and Micha were giving her conflicting advice. She was arguing with them as they walked along.

'He'll never take me with him to see the Count,' she argued. 'It's the most important thing in the world to him. Much more important than me,' she finished forlornly.

Azaz spoke.

'I can't just *make* him,' she snapped.

Blanco wasn't listening to her as his mind was filled with the thought of the flying machine and also the letters that Gump had told him about. Since his ship had been attacked by pirates he had barely had any time to himself to think. The letters he puzzled over for a while. He would have to find a way of getting them back. He felt guilty that he might have to steal them but then, he comforted himself, if the Count had stolen them first, it wasn't really stealing if he just took them back; and if they were Gump's personal letters then the Count should never have taken them in the first place. He shook his head to clear his mind. He would worry about that when he got there. Instead he turned his thoughts to the flying machine. A shiver of pure delight ran through him as he thought that soon he would be working with the Count on it.

★   ★   ★

The Count was also thinking about the flying machine. He was stuck. He had been stuck for months. He had lost count of the number of servants he had lost to the trials. He had eventually had to give up using them before he had no one left to serve him his dinner. That was why he had sent the letter to Blanco. He had met Blanco the previous summer when he had gone to Venice on business. Everyone had talked about Signor Taddei and the problems that he had with his son. Instead of learning the family business he preferred to spend most of his days playing with pieces of wood and jumping off tall buildings. And when he wasn't doing that, he was spending time with his great-uncle Marco, whom many people thought of as a liar, or at least as an inspired fabricator of stories. The Count sneered as he thought of Marco. They had a long history, he and Marco Polo. It wasn't only in Malta that they had met, although he doubted that Marco remembered the earlier time. He wondered if the old fool was missing his letters yet. No matter what he thought, Magdalena had never been his.

The Count had been intrigued by the sound of the boy, Blanco, and also by the coincidental fact that he was related to his old adversary. He was happy to interfere in his life—if only for the sake of annoying Marco. But he had also needed someone who understood his interest in flying machines. When he saw Blanco's experiments—and the boy had been delighted to find someone interested in them—

he had thought that the boy had something in
his designs. He had a flair for it in a way that
the Count did not. Maybe because flying was
not the Count's sole interest as it was Blanco's.

After much discussion with the others, he
finally sent for Blanco.

How Blanco found himself agreeing to take Eva with
him to meet the Count was a question that he could
never answer in the future. He thought that it was
probably because she had pleaded for days—over the
mountains, crossing streams, through dusty plains,
and he was almost certain that she actually invaded
his sleep. Finally, in order to achieve some peace,
and to return to his dreams of flying uninterrupted,
he had agreed.

While Blanco would never say that they were
friends, he was beginning to enjoy Eva's almost
incessant chatter. The journey, he realized, would
have been fairly boring without her. They traipsed
for days when all they could see was the dry, dusty
road in front of them and her talking made it pass by
all the quicker. Most of the villagers they met were
nice enough. They were always willing to sell them
food and often a place to sleep—a barn more often
than not—but he found none of the celebrations or
great hospitality that his uncle had mentioned so
often in his book.

Blanco had never seen a country with so much
dust, nor so hot. They often gave up and fell asleep
during the early part of the afternoon and walked for
longer into the cool of the evening. They slept out
under the stars most nights for their funds were

growing low, although they were always careful to build a large fire. And through it all Eva talked about everything—except for her family and her angels. Her family Blanco had never heard her mention, apart from that one time about the stars, and she had stopped talking about her angels when he forbade her. He would sigh and turn away in disgust whenever she said their names.

'Tell me about your family,' he said, breaking into a long tale about why she loved the colour red so much. 'You never talk about them.'

They had sat down beside a stream to eat the food that they had bought from a village a while back. Bread and cheese again, Blanco had thought as he paid for it. He would be happy if he never saw cheese again. They had been given some olives as well which made a welcome change, but what he wouldn't give to sit down in front of a plate of roasted meats. It was to take his mind off this that he had asked Eva about her family.

' . . . and it's the colour of blood,' she finished as he interrupted her with his question. She paused and glanced at him without replying to his question. She had no intention of talking about her family. She was still too angry about them sending her off to a foreign country to be married. Then she looked at him properly. He was lying on his back, squinting through the branches of the tree above him and looking as though he didn't have a care in the world. He was no longer the tidy, fashionably dressed boy that she had met on the ship. His hair was longer and was stuck together with dust. His clothes were torn and had changed from what had once been a bright peacock blue to an indistinguishable greyish brown. His face was thinner and covered in dirt. She looked down at herself. Her dress, too, was torn and dirty. Without much more ado she started to take it off.

'Eva?' asked Blanco when the silence grew too long. He was still staring up at the sky and it wasn't until he heard a splash that he looked around. The first thing that he saw was a pair of boots lying on their sides as though they had just been tossed there. Another splash made him sit up and turn his attention to the stream. There was someone in it.

'Eva?' he cried in horror. 'Eva, what are you doing?'

'Bathing,' she replied happily. She was lying on the bed of the shallow stream, leaning on her hands. Blanco could see only her head.

'Do you think that's a good idea?' he asked hesitantly.

'I think it's an excellent idea,' she replied turning over so that she was floating on her back. 'It's lovely and cool and I can get all the dust out of my hair.' She kicked her legs a little. 'You should try it,' she added. 'You look terribly dusty yourself.'

Blanco wasn't a huge fan of bathing and his experiences with water so far on this trip had not been very enjoyable. Still, it did look lovely and cool and he was terribly hot and dusty. The sun glinted on the stream so that it looked all silvery, as if little diamonds were glittering on the surface. For a moment he was reminded of the Count's eyes and he had to blink to get the image to go away.

'Where's your dress?' he asked after looking round to see where it was.

'In here,' she said, sitting up and holding it in front of her. 'I thought it needed a wash too.'

Blanco blushed furiously as he realized that Eva must be dressed only in her underclothes. He paused. 'I'll . . . I'll just wait till you come back out,' he said.

'Don't be silly!' cried Eva. 'Just come in. I promise I won't look!' And, true to her word, she dipped her head under the water and swam away.

Blanco couldn't wait a moment longer. He realized just how hot, dirty, and probably smelly he was. He tore off his outer clothes and ran into the stream—a suitably modest distance away from Eva—and sank down into its cool silky waters. He ducked his head under and scrubbed at his hair and then turned and floated on his back as he had seen Eva do. The stream was shallow enough that he could rest his hands on the bottom, to balance himself as he lay there.

'Isn't it glorious?' asked Eva.

'Beautiful,' replied Blanco. In truth, he didn't think he had ever felt so happy in all his life. To have been so hot and dusty and then, in a matter of moments, to have that washed away and to lie in this cool, silvery water while still feeling the sun beating down and warming his limbs was a mixture of sensations that he could never have believed possible. This, he thought, was pure rapture.

They stayed there for most of the afternoon. They washed their clothes and laid them out on bushes to dry and then returned to the stream to lie there and talk. It was an afternoon that they would both look back on with much pleasure when things got difficult later. It also wasn't until much later that Blanco realized that she still hadn't told him about her family.

'Stop smiling, Micha,' said Azaz. 'The difficult part hasn't even begun yet.'

They were watching Blanco and Eva in the stream. They were playing a game, splashing at each other and laughing. They were like two young children playing, all thoughts of marriage and plans flown away for the moment. The angels were perched high up in the tree, Micha leaning against the trunk and Azaz lying full length along one of the branches.

'You thought we'd never even get them together,' replied Micha calmly. 'You thought that he would get rid of her with the pilgrims.'

Azaz scratched his ear and smiled. 'I was wrong,' he said simply. 'I underestimated you.'

'Not me,' said Micha. 'Love.'

Azaz looked at her sharply at that. 'It's not love,' he said abruptly. 'Blanco still sees her as a hindrance, as a mere duty that he has to get rid of.'

'At the moment,' said Micha.

'Be careful, Micha,' said Azaz. 'Don't put all your hopes on to them. We've a serious task ahead. I don't want you sidetracked by some romantic notion of love and happy endings.'

'What about you?' said Micha. 'You have an ulterior motive too.'

Azaz grinned. 'But I don't believe in happy endings,' he said.

Chapter 7

They saw the castle long before they saw the village that lay beneath it. It stood proud in the distance, the tower a large dark finger pointing up to the heavens. The cliff that it stood on was sheer and had been carved out of the surrounding countryside as though by a giant knife. From first sight to arriving in the village, it took three days' travelling.

Griffin was the first to see them. He had been leaning on the battlements looking out, wishing that he was down in the village having a goblet of wine and sharing some laughs with the men. He had not left the castle for over three years. He sighed. That was the sacrifice he had to make for world domination, he supposed.

There were two paths which approached the foot of the cliff. One led to the village which was directly below the castle, at the bottom of the cliff, and the other curved round the back of the cliff, to climb up to the castle. As Griffin watched he saw two small figures approaching. They were still a fair distance from the crossroads.

Griffin jumped to his feet. They must have made fast progress from the stream, for his

*master had calculated that they would not be
here for another couple of days. He leaned out
over the battlements and almost fell over when
a hand was placed on his back. That selfsame
hand jerked him back in.*

*'Master,' grovelled Griffin, kissing the hem
of his master's robe. He dared not look up.
'He's still got the girl with him.'*

*'Go and get them, Griffin,' said his master's
voice. 'They must not reach the village. We'll
deal with the girl later.'*

'There's a crossroads up ahead,' said Blanco. 'It
looks like we can go to the village or straight to the
castle.'

'Oh, let's go to the village first,' said Eva. 'I'm not
sure I'm ready to meet a count yet. I think I should
have a bath or something.'

Blanco smiled at her. Since their afternoon at the
stream, he had felt much happier about taking her to
the castle with him. It made him sad sometimes, the
thought of her marrying an old man, but he really
could see no alternative. She wouldn't return to
Venice and he couldn't just leave her. 'He's really
not that kind of count,' he said. 'I don't think he'll
be bothered about a little dust.' Although as he said
this, he remembered that the Count had always
looked impeccably tidy.

Blanco looked up at the castle after he finished
speaking. He couldn't control a shiver of pleasure at
the sight of the tower. It was so high. This could be
it, he felt. He could finally achieve a successful flight.
With that kind of height, how could he possibly fail?

'It's more than a little dust,' said Eva forlornly, tugging at her dress. In reality, she wasn't that bothered about how she looked. She was worried about the Count and the castle. Ever since they had seen it three days before, Blanco had talked of nothing but flying and his excitement at building a flying machine. She felt that her time at the castle was going to be very boring and she still didn't like the sound of the Count. But at least, she supposed, it was better than getting married. She could only hope that Azaz and Micha would come back soon or she would be terribly lonely. They had left her once the castle was in sight.

'There's someone coming,' said Blanco, 'along the road from the castle.'

They both stopped and stared at the apparition coming towards them. It was running but its knees were almost hitting the ground at every stride as though it was so tired it was almost falling over. It was hard to distinguish anything else for it was completely covered in rags; every hair of its head (if it had any) to over the bottom of its feet was covered in rags in every shade of brown. They watched in amazement as it approached them, fully expecting it to pass them. When it finally halted in front of them and spoke, they realized that it was, indeed, a man.

'Come, come.' He flapped his arms at them. His nose was the only feature visible on his face for it stuck out through the cloths. His voice was muffled but his meaning was clear.

Blanco and Eva stared at each other.

'Do you think he's from the Count?' asked Eva in wonder.

Griffin recognized the word 'Count' and nodded

vigorously. He put out a cloth-covered hand and placed it on Eva's arm and made a tugging movement.

'Count, Count,' he said. 'Come, come.'

Eva laughed. 'I suppose that's our decision made for us,' she said.

She chattered to Griffin as they set off along the path to the castle. Blanco followed along quietly behind, lost in his thoughts. Soon his dream was about to come true. He hoped that the Count didn't mind that he had brought Eva with him. Would he get to fly straight away? He shook his head as he realized that was unlikely—after all, the Count had invited him because he was having problems with the machine. And how was he to get Gump's letters back off the Count without him finding out?

Full as his head was with these thoughts it took Blanco a while to realize that his was not the only voice he could hear in his head. He appeared to have been joined there by someone who insisted his name was Azaz.

The Count was in the courtyard waiting to greet them. He was exactly as Blanco remembered him, from his glimmering grey eyes right down to the silvery cloak which swung around his ankles. Blanco spared a thought for Gump's pickled quinces as he looked at it. He was even taller than Blanco had remembered and he was almost as thin as Eva's Aunt Hildegard. Blanco tried not to think any further about her. He still felt guilty about leaving her to almost certain death with those pirates.

'Blanco, my dear boy!' said the Count, coming forward to greet him and enveloping him in the cloak. Blanco smelt a strange earthy aroma, mixed with an exotic spicy redolence, before he was released again. 'It is so delightful to see you here. I cannot thank you enough for coming.' His eyes glittered in a disturbing manner and Blanco could not hold their gaze for long. He felt as though the Count was trying to see into his soul. He was also uncomfortably aware of his somewhat dishevelled appearance. What had appeared unimportant on the road was shown up next to the Count's dapper clothing. But nothing could truly disturb his delight and excitement that he had, at last, reached his destination.

'I'm so happy to be here,' he said. 'I had one or two adventures on the way but I knew I'd get here in the end.'

'Nothing too traumatic, I hope,' murmured the Count in a sympathetic tone. 'Nothing life threatening.'

'No, no, nothing like that,' said Blanco, looking around him and so happy to be here that he felt as though he had only left Venice yesterday, rather than months before. 'I would have walked through fire for this chance anyway,' he said looking excitedly at the Count. 'I was so excited when I received your letter.'

'And your father didn't mind you taking the trip?' asked the Count smoothly.

Blanco hesitated. Should he tell the truth? But then, what if Count Maleficio sent him back? 'He was delighted,' he said. 'He said that it is always important to have good relations with trading partners.'

'He said I was his trading partner?' queried the Count, raising an eyebrow. 'Interesting.'

Too late, Blanco realized that he didn't actually know what business the Count had had with his father. He had only guessed that it was to do with trade. He babbled on.

'He's very pleased for me. I've been sending him letters all the way.'

As he said this, he felt a pang of guilt for he had sent no letters to anyone since he left Venice. Certainly not to his father, but not to his mother or to Gump either. His mother must be frantic with worry. He could only hope that Gump would have told her something of his plans.

Eva had been looking around the courtyard as this exchange took place. It was relatively small but since she had never been inside a castle before she found it very interesting. Three sides of it were two floors high and were built of a grey stone which seemed to soak up the very light of the sun. The fourth wall held the tower and it was built of a smooth black stone. The tower itself blocked out the sun and caused a large shadow to fall into the courtyard. She thought how clever it was that everything was protected by the thick outer walls and by the large iron portcullis which had been lifted as they approached. It was like having a little town in one building.

'And who is this *charming* young lady?' asked the Count, turning his metal grey eyes on Eva. Suddenly shy, she shrank back against Blanco, terrified that the Count would try to embrace her too. She was a little scared of him. It was as though he had no bones but rather was just a shimmering mass of molten metal. She could tell that he really wasn't very pleased to see her although he would never admit it.

'This is Eva,' said Blanco, a little nervously. 'I hope you don't mind me bringing her but I have to take her to Barcelona and this was on the way.'

'Not at all, not at all,' said the Count, taking one of Eva's hands and holding it in between both of his. 'It is a pleasure to have female company. We don't have very much of it around here.'

He was interrupted by a cough behind him. They all turned to see a woman there and the Count waved her forward.

'Good day,' said the woman. 'I'm Godoffel, the housekeeper. I'll show you to your rooms.'

Blanco and Eva could not take their eyes from her. She was a monstrously huge woman who possessed more chins than either of them could count on both hands. On each chin she had a wart which increased in size the nearer they got to her face, so that on what was probably her original chin, she had one the size of a clenched fist. This wobbled ominously when she spoke. It seemed to have a life of its own and continued to move even after she had stopped speaking. Blanco noticed, when he finally managed to remove his eyes from the lower part of her face, that she had almost no hair. She had only a few wisps that straggled untidily across her bald pate—about the same amount of hair as the number of teeth she had in her mouth, although they seemed barely worth keeping, ground down as they were to yellowing, decaying stumps.

'Go with Godoffel. She's the housekeeper. She'll show you to your rooms,' said the Count, seemingly ignoring their rude staring. 'Come and find me later in the tower room.'

Still staring, Blanco and Eva bade their farewells and followed Godoffel to the entrance to the block opposite the tower wall. Only when they were plunged into the gloom inside did they finally blink.

Eva reached for Blanco's hand as they clambered up dark stairs behind the housekeeper. They were lit only by the tiniest of slits in the thick walls and even the strong white-hot sunlight could not penetrate them.

She led them along a corridor and finally stopped in front of a large wooden door.

'The boy goes in here,' she said, throwing it open. They both peeped in. At least it was lighter for it had a large window. Also, to Blanco's joy, it looked on to the tower. He could dream of flying from it even when he was lying in bed. The bed itself was large and sumptuous.

'And the girl here,' she pointed to a door across the corridor.

She turned and left without showing them into Eva's room. Blanco and Eva made a face at each other and then threw open the door to her room.

'Oh,' said Eva.

'Oh,' said Blanco.

The room was delightful. It was gorgeously decorated in reds and golds and the huge bed was hung with pink velvet curtains. There were sweet-meats on a table and, most exciting of all to Eva, lying across the bed there was a beautiful dress in deep emerald green with gold threads. The green was a perfect match for her eyes. She rushed over and picked it up.

'Oh, this is so beautiful!' she cried. 'Look, Blanco!' She held up the dress to herself and twirled round, showing it off. 'I've never seen such a lovely dress.'

Blanco had crossed the room and was looking out of the window.

'Eva,' he said. 'Come and look at this.'

Eva broke off from twirling her dress and joined him at the window.

'Look at that!' Blanco pointed downwards.

They could see the village from where they stood. It lay straggled about the hillside like countless other villages they had passed on their journeying. But Blanco was pointing at a hole which lay right in the centre of it. It was large and untidy looking and looked utterly incongruous in the middle of the street.

'What do you think that is?' he asked.

'A quarry, maybe?' Eva replied, her mind still fixated on her dress. What did she care for large holes in the middle of villages? She had a nice comfortable bed to sleep in for the first time in weeks, a good meal to come, and a new dress to wear.

It never crossed either of their minds to wonder why the dress was there or how the Count had known that she was coming.

'Hello,' said Azaz.

'Who are you?'

'I'm Azaz,' said Azaz. 'I'm one of Eva's angels.'

'But I don't believe in angels.'

'Then maybe you have been touched by the moon.'

A pause.

'Why can't I see you? Eva says that she can see you when you talk.'

Azaz laughed. Blanco felt a warm puff of air caressing his neck but when he turned round there was still nothing there.

'What are you doing?' asked Eva impatiently. 'Why are you doing a turn halfway up the stairs?'

They were on their way up to the tower room to find the Count. Eva couldn't wait to thank him for the dress and Blanco was keen to find out how the flying machine was looking. It had taken them a while to find the entrance to the tower. After the excitement of their rooms and after Eva had freshened herself up a little—'I think the Count deserves that we wash our faces, at least'—they decided to go. They managed to find their way back down to the courtyard. Once there, however, they took the door that they thought led up to the tower and found themselves in the kitchen instead.

This was a huge room full of much activity. Godoffel sat in a large chair at the far end, with her feet up against an enormous fireplace in which the largest fire that Blanco had ever seen was lit. Over it was a whole pig, its flesh popping with fat, being turned on a spit by a small boy whose face was so red it looked painful. The tables were loaded with a huge variety of food. There were piles of fruit of all shapes and varieties—small, furry apricots; green, gleaming apples; peeled oranges; and armfuls of grapes. There were bowls full of what looked to Eva's delighted eyes to be cake and a large fowl stood in the centre, waiting to be carved. There were five or six people cutting, mixing, stirring, or chopping and not one of them paid any attention to the two in the doorway.

Blanco's mouth watered and he took an involuntary step forward. Eva stopped him. 'I think this is probably our dinner,' she whispered. 'Maybe we should wait until then.'

'Just one little piece of bread or a chicken leg,' replied Blanco. 'That's all I need.'

It had been with difficulty that Eva had turned him away from the kitchen but once they had found the correct entrance to the tower his thoughts soon turned back to the flying machine.

He had been halfway up the stairs when Azaz had spoken to him. He had been aware of the voice for some time but he had continued ignoring it; but this time he had replied—not out loud, of course. He didn't want Eva to hear him after he had told her so emphatically that he did not believe in her angels. And, anyway, he still wasn't completely convinced and when Eva spoke he decided he had been imagining things again.

'I thought I felt something against my neck,' he said. He gave a quick glance round again but no, still nothing there. 'Come on,' he said. 'Let's keep going.'

'There are so many steps,' moaned Eva. 'How many more, do you think?'

'How should I know?' asked Blanco. 'I've not been here before. It looked pretty high from the outside though, so I should say that we still have a long way to go.'

Eva sighed and put her head down. She had lost count after the first hundred or so. Her legs were aching and her feet felt so heavy as she lifted them on to each new step. She didn't think that she would be making this trip very often. She would leave it to the Count and Blanco.

Finally, gasping for breath, they reached a door and Blanco pulled on the big bell pull. Seconds later the door opened and a beaming Count Maleficio greeted them.

'You made it!' he cried. 'It's hard work, isn't it? But still, I like to think it's worth it. Come in! Come in!'

He stepped back, allowing Blanco and Eva to step in to the room. He slammed the door shut behind them. Once there they were so overcome by amazement that they said nothing. Only their heavy breathing could be heard.

There appeared to be no window in the room. The sides were totally dark but the room itself was not for it was lit, not with torches and candles, but with a multitude of stars scattered across the ceiling. Eva and Blanco stood in delight and amazement, staring at them as they winked and blinked. Blanco could even recognize some of the groupings. It was like looking straight at the night sky.

'Blanco,' whispered Eva, awed and maybe just a little frightened. 'It is still day, isn't it?'

'I think so,' Blanco whispered back.

The Count laughed. 'Do you like it?' he asked in a delighted voice. 'It's one of my little experiments.' His voice came from the far side of the room and the next instant he drew back some thick black curtains and bright sunlight was in Eva's face. Instantly, the stars disappeared.

'That was amazing,' breathed out Blanco. 'Beautiful. How did you do that?'

The Count laughed in delight and waved a hand round the room. 'This is my playroom, you might say.'

The room was filled with a spectrum of delights. Experiments at all stages were scattered throughout the room. Strange smells assaulted their nostrils at every turn. There was something burning over on the far side and right next to Eva were pieces of metal and rocks, all twisted together as though an experiment had gone far wrong. One piece of equipment was quite obviously an astrolabe for Blanco had seen one before, and he pointed it out to Eva, although even Blanco had never seen such a glorious one as this. It was made of some kind of gleaming metal (gold, Blanco thought, but that seemed such extravagance) and was covered with intricate carvings and markings. He looked at it for only a moment before his eye was caught by what he correctly guessed to be a water clock. This was an extraordinary piece of machinery which was supposed to be able to tell the exact time. He had never seen one before and gently stroked its mechanisms and could have played with it for hours had his attention not been caught by something much more important.

They lay over in the far corner, next to one of the windows—a range of machines, all of which were undeniably built to fly. The Count saw the direction in which his eyes had gone and he grabbed hold of his hand and dragged him over.

'What do you think of birds?' he said.

'Birds?' queried Blanco.

'Mmm. What do you think their tails are for?'

'Tails?'

The Count's silvery eyes glittered, half in impatience and half in excitement.

His question was a good one and one that Blanco hadn't thought about much himself.

'I suppose,' he thought hard for a moment, 'I suppose that they're for balance.'

'No, no!' cried the Count excitedly. 'I knew you'd say that!'

'Then, what?' asked Blanco, instantly caught up in the excitement of the flying machines and forgetting about everything else in the room. The wonder of the night stars appearing inside, Eva, the water clock, everything faded beside the idea of flying.

If Eva had wondered whether Blanco really wanted to fly and was willing to risk his life for the chance to do so, she had her answer now. His eyes glittered, his mouth was stretched into a permanent smile, and he was completely engrossed in talking to the Count. She gave a rueful little smile and turned to explore what else lay in the room.

A beautiful chart lay spread out across the table against which she was leaning. It was filled with little drawings, lines, and names. Eva had never seen such a beautifully drawn astrological chart before. She started to read it.

'*Azaz! There's another one of us here. It's Rameel.*'

Azaz almost fell off the wings of the flying machine where he was lying stretched out listening to Count Maleficio and Blanco discuss how best to correct its faults. He had been amazed that they had worked out that birds needed their tails not for balance, but in order to land properly.

As he caught himself he noticed that Eva was staring at them. He was fairly sure that she couldn't see them, but she obviously knew that they were there. He motioned to Micha and they left the room.

'*How do you know?*' *he asked.*

'*I saw him,*' *replied Micha. Her voice was low and*

trembling. 'He must know we're here. Why has he not come forward?'

'Because he is a coward,' replied Azaz fiercely. 'He always was.'

'I think this could get dangerous,' said Micha. 'Maybe we should persuade Eva to leave?'

Azaz shook his head. 'We knew that there was something happening here,' he said. 'We can't change all the plans now.'

'Maybe Rameel has changed,' said Micha hopefully.

Azaz smiled but it wasn't a pleasant one. 'Let's find out,' he said.

Chapter 8

At home, both Blanco and Eva had been used to a large variety of food. Venice being a trading port, its citizens had access to most of the items which were traded within its confines and beyond. Salt, spices, new varieties of fruit and vegetables from the Middle East, the Far East, and the neighbouring countries were all available to even the lowest of Venetian citizens should they be able to afford them. But nothing could have prepared them for the delicacies and varieties which were on offer at the dinner table that day. Even Eva was, for once, struck speechless.

The first course, the Count informed them, was made up of dishes from the southern part of Spain. There was a stuffed capon and pork swimming in a spicy sauce. They could smell apricots and saffron, cloves and ginger, pepper and cinnamon and for every spice there was a meat or fish dish marinating in it.

The Count lifted the lid off one of the large silver dishes and breathed in the aroma which escaped.

'Aaah,' he said, closing his eyes and leaning back in his chair. 'Couscous.'

Blanco had never had couscous before although he had heard much about it and he was quite disappointed when he looked at it and it was some kind of porridge-style dish. Since the Count thought it such a delicacy he forced himself to take some. It was a succulent yellow in colour and when he bent down to smell it, its aroma was of strange hot spices. After looking his fill, he picked some up and gingerly tasted it. The flavour which immediately flooded his mouth exceeded all his expectations—though it had to be said that they weren't very high in the first place. He hurriedly put another two or three handfuls on to his plate in case it all disappeared although there must have been enough to feed fifty people. He enjoyed the second mouthful almost more than the first. Then he started to try all the dishes on the table. All kinds of meats, fruits, and vegetables— venison, lamb, beef, whole stuffed fish, chicken, pomegranates, onions, spiced pies, and sweet pastries flavoured with almonds soon filled his plate. There was a flavour of everything that he had ever tasted and some new ones besides.

There were two other things unusual about the meal although Blanco didn't notice them until the second course was brought in. The first was that their trenchers were made not of bread but of metal; in fact, of silver which felt slightly strange. Blanco found that food just didn't taste the same when eaten from it.

The second unusual thing came along with the second course and that was a three-pronged instrument with which they were supposed to stab their meat to bring it from the platters to their own personal trenchers. Count Maleficio informed them with delight that the implement was called a fork and showed them how to use it.

'It really is *most* delightful,' he explained. 'As well as procuring the meat,' and he stabbed his fork into a steaming piece of beef, 'one can also use it to help to cut it up on one's trencher.'

And he put his fork into the meat on his trencher till all three prongs were sunk into it and proceeded to cut a small piece of meat off the end. What he did next was even more strange for he removed his fork from the larger piece of the meat and put it into the smaller part and then carried it to his mouth and popped it inside.

Blanco looked at Eva and she looked as amazed as he did. Blanco looked down at the small fork that he held in his right hand and thought that he might give it a try.

He carefully followed every movement that the Count had made but with much less success for as soon as he started to cut his meat it shot forward off his trencher and landed on the table.

The Count laughed in a friendly manner and Eva joined in with him, though she made no effort to try it herself and she was still a little unsure about the Count.

'It's not as easy as it looks, is it?' asked the Count.

Blanco shook his head as he glumly speared the meat and placed it back on his trencher.

'Well, I'm not even going to try,' said Eva, picking up her chicken leg and gnawing on it, delighting in the juice as it dripped down her chin. 'This is a much more sensible way to eat.'

Luckily Blanco was saved from his dilemma by the Count putting down his fork and picking up his meat and eating it in the normal way. Blanco therefore gnawed away quite happily on all his meat dishes, throwing the bones over his shoulder on to the floor as he had done all his life. Until Eva kicked him under the table and indicated the large bowl in the middle of the table which had been empty when the meal had commenced and which was now full of bones.

'Sorry,' cried Blanco, leaping to his feet and dropping down into the sweet-smelling rushes behind his chair. 'I'll just pick them all back up.'

'Leave them,' the Count said, chuckling. 'Griffin will pick them up later.'

Griffin was just entering with the third course at this point and gave a heavy sigh at this. Blanco sat back down in his chair, red of face and somewhat ashamed. However, he soon forgot his discomfiture as he laid eyes on the delights offered by the third course.

Along with this course came a small, smiling, white-haired man who sat down at the opposite end of the table from the Count. Count Maleficio looked startled for a moment and then smiled benignly down the table at his new guest.

'Blanco, Eva,' he said, waving towards the man, 'this is another guest who is staying here. He's an old friend of mine from Granada, Señor . . .'

'I do hope you don't mind my intrusion,' bellowed out the Stranger. 'I have quite recovered from my earlier indisposition and thought I would join you after all. You never mentioned that there would be such a charming lady companion.'

Here he beamed at Eva, who blushed and didn't know quite what to say in return. He patted her on the arm and turned his attentions to what lay on the dinner table.

'Count Maleficio,' asked Eva suddenly, after cocking her head to one side in an action that Blanco knew well. 'Why is there a large hole in the middle of the village?'

Blanco and Eva both agreed later that they must have imagined the sudden chill in the room. Griffin had just opened the door and a draught must have entered with him. The small man had laughed.

'The hole, my dear?' asked the Count, his grey eyes narrowing. 'I think it used to be a quarry. I'm not sure. It's been there much longer than I have.'

The Count, he had informed them earlier, had only acquired the castle a couple of years before. He had been drawn to it because of the exceptionally high tower which he had thought would be perfect for his flying experiments.

Eva was flummoxed. She was sure that the hole was not a quarry but she could not say so without appearing rude.

The Stranger leaned across the table. 'That dress looks wonderful on you, my dear,' he said to Eva. 'It's just your colour. And it matches your eyes perfectly.'

Eva beamed with pleasure. Having never been a particularly attractive child—and suffering additionally from having an exceptionally beautiful elder sister—she was always happy to hear compliments and the man sounded very sincere. She glanced over at Blanco to see if he was going to add anything but he was still pondering his fork. He asked the Count to explain the design. Eva sighed and turned back to the Stranger who was more than delighted to talk to her.

Blanco was in a quandary. The Count was being so

hospitable and friendly and sharing all his flying secrets with him and Blanco was planning to rob him.

'I promise you,' he could almost hear Gump's voice still echoing in his head. 'Those letters are mine. The Count can charm you all he likes. You may even feel guilty about taking them. But, remember, Blanco. He took them from me first.'

Blanco turned over yet again in his bed. He was restless. Torn between guilt at what he was planning to do to the Count and suffering a little from the excessive amount of dinner he had eaten, he was finding sleep difficult. He kicked at his covers like a baby. He sat up and gazed out of the window. He had left the shutters open and now he looked upon the tower. It rose high into the sky, dark, mysterious and full of secrets.

The steps were cold against his bare feet. Why hadn't he thought to put on some shoes? He was nearly at the top so there was no point in going back for them now.

He hadn't meant to go to the tower. He had thought to go down to the kitchens for some mint. His stomach was grumbling quite a lot now and he knew from Bella that mint eased its aching. But once outside his door his feet turned, almost of their own accord, towards the tower.

As he approached the door he had a sudden horror that it might be locked. Had he come all this way for nothing? He reached out and pushed it and was very relieved when it swung open, albeit with a loud creak.

He wasn't sure who got the biggest surprise. He himself almost fell back down the stairs while Eva looked as though she were about to faint.

'What are you doing here?' he hissed.

Rameel was grooming himself in the mirror when the two angels materialized behind him. He did not look surprised to see them.

'Azaz. Micha,' he greeted them, bowing his head to each reflection. Not even by a blink of an eye did he betray any emotion that he might be feeling. 'It's been a long time.'

The angels did not reply.

'Some would say too long,' he continued still gazing at them from the mirror. He turned round. 'I wouldn't be one of them.'

Azaz bowed his head in acknowledgement of the declaration of hostilities. Micha looked upset but resigned.

Rameel smoothed down his dark purple tunic. His wings were long, much longer than either Azaz's or Micha's but they were thin and curled round to the front to cover his feet. They were dark like a crow's and looked as though they needed to be picked clean. His long, dark hair, Azaz noted, was braided with thin gold strands but the greasiness was apparent. In addition, the yellow of the gold only enhanced the sallowness of his face. His eyes blazed with tigerish wrath—the only ray of light in his body. Azaz was sure that that was how he too, must have looked when he first returned to earth. By contrast, Micha's golden face and his obsidian one now glowed with health and vitality.

'What are you doing here, Rameel?' asked Azaz. 'I thought you were still . . . ' he searched for the right word, 'elsewhere.'

'I was released.' Rameel threw his arms into the air in a gesture of triumph. 'I said I was sorry. I served my time.' He paused and then added, 'As did you.'

'I'm still serving,' snapped Azaz. 'I learnt my lesson. It would appear that you did not.'

Rameel ignored him and turned to Micha. 'You look as beautiful as ever, Micha. Fallen in love lately?' His voice was malicious.

Micha looked at him haughtily. 'At least I know what love is,' she replied calmly. 'You still haven't told us why you're here.'

Rameel spread his arms wide. 'Why,' he said. 'This is my home. Where else would I be? The question surely is, why are *you* here?'

Blanco and Eva made themselves comfortable underneath the windowsill, wrapping themselves in the window coverings for warmth. Once they had got over the shock of finding each other where neither of them should be, they had decided to find somewhere comfortable to sit before telling each other their stories.

'You first,' said Blanco.

'That's unfair,' said Eva and then stopped. She supposed it maybe wasn't that unfair since Blanco could have a semi-legitimate reason for being in the tower room whereas she had none. But she knew that Blanco wouldn't like the answer.

'Micha told me to come,' she said. 'She wanted me to look around for her.'

Blanco did not sigh as he normally did whenever she mentioned the angels. He remained quiet, so quiet, in fact, that Eva felt she had to keep talking. 'I don't know why she couldn't just come herself but she said she had something to do. I don't know what. She doesn't always tell me everything. I think—'

But what Eva thought remained forever a mystery for Blanco interrupted her. 'What does it sound like when they talk to you? How do you know that they're there?'

'Who?' said Eva. 'Oh. The angels, you mean?'

She leaned back, brushing against Blanco's bare arm as she did so. He felt warm. She snuggled a little closer to get some heat.

'Yes,' he said. 'Can you hear them?'

'When they want me to.'

'Do they always agree with each other?'

'Not always.' She laughed in remembrance. 'Sometimes they fight over me. One day when I was out riding with my cousins I wanted to try it without wearing my skirts. My cousin Roberto lent me some of his clothing and we went out riding. Azaz thought it was a great idea but Micha didn't. She said it was very unladylike. They had a full blown argument and ended up pulling me off my horse.'

'How could they pull you off the horse?' Blanco asked sceptically.

'It was like they were tugging me in separate directions,' she explained. 'Micha pulled very hard when Azaz had let go and I fell off.' She giggled. 'You should have seen Roberto's face. One minute I was sitting on my horse and the next I was lying on the ground. He thought I'd been struck by something.'

'Does Roberto know about Azaz and Micha?'

'Oh yes. He thought they were funny. He thought I was funny.' She had quite a wistful look on her face as she talked of her cousin and Blanco felt a sudden kick of what could possibly be described as jealousy. He shook himself to get rid of such a ridiculous feeling.

'So they can touch you?'

'Sometimes. Not often. I don't think they like to touch me. It makes them sad. I can see them, though,' she said. 'I've told you that before. Azaz is very tall, his face is a kind of shiny black, and he always wears red. And Micha is also very tall but she's dressed completely in white and has long blonde hair and a kind of golden face. And, of course, they both have wings.'

'Can you always see them?'

'No, if they don't want me to then I can't.' She hesitated for a moment, wondering if she should say about them deliberately hiding from her this afternoon in the tower room. She decided not to bother. She turned her head to try to see Blanco but the room was impossibly dark. She jumped up and tugged at one of the shutters letting in some of the moonlight.

'Wasn't that amazing today with the stars?' she asked dreamily, leaning out of the window, looking up at the real ones. 'I really thought that the Count had made night come early.'

Blanco stood up and leant out beside her. He looked down but could see nothing but the darkness. He was just about to tell Eva about hearing Azaz when she said:

'But what are you doing here?' She smiled. 'You really love it, don't you?'

Blanco was sidetracked instantly. 'Oh yes,' he said, wandering over and stroking the sides of the machine that was in the nearest state to completion. 'And I think we're going to be able to make it fly, too.' He hesitated. 'But that's not why I'm here,' he said.

Eva had come to stand beside him. She reached out a hand to the machine as well. Now that she was here she could understand Blanco's desire to fly—although she had no wish to try it for herself! Launching herself from the tower window and gliding down to the ground far below was the fabric of Eva's nightmares rather than her dreams.

'Micha told me that you would come up here tonight,' she said eventually. 'She said I should help you find the letters.'

Blanco turned to her in surprise and not a little anger. 'How do you *do* that?' he asked. 'How do you know everything that's going to happen next?'

Eva bit her lip and looked downcast. This always happened. This was why she wasn't sure that the angels weren't a curse rather than a blessing. People really didn't like having their every move second-guessed.

'If it makes you feel any better,' she said, 'I don't know what they are for or who or anything about them really. Micha just said that you might need some help.'

'Well, I suppose . . . ' he started grudgingly. 'Look,' he continued, 'I don't feel very happy about sneaking about in the Count's study—he's been very good to invite me here and let me work with him, so just don't touch anything but the letters.'

Eva nodded enthusiastically in agreement and crossed the room before he could change his mind.

'It is all rather amazing,' she said, wandering around. 'For such a creepy man, he does have some good ideas.'

'He's not creepy,' said Blanco, as he searched among the shelves at the far end of the room. 'He's very clever.'

'Really?' said Eva, as she peered at a jar containing what looked like an assortment of fingernails. In the light of the candle which she held they gleamed ghoulishly in their jar. She wandered over to the large table where she had been earlier that day and spotted the astrological chart that she had been looking at. She perused it again and eventually called Blanco over.

'What?' he asked crossly. He had been distracted by reading a manual about how to create optical illusions and didn't want to be interrupted.

'It's this,' she said. 'I don't like the look of it.'

'It looks like a map,' said Blanco, looking at all the strange characters inscribed on it.

'It's not a map,' explained Eva. 'It's an astrological chart. I think it's the Count's. And I think this is meant to be you.'

She pointed to a character who was offering a hand.

'This is you being a saviour,' she explained.

Blanco puffed his chest a little with pride. 'I knew the Count couldn't build the flying machine without me,' he said. 'With his tools and my knowledge we should manage, but without me . . . '

'But that means,' said Eva, 'that this is you too.' And she pointed to a character who looked as though he was suffering agonies, with large spikes sticking out of every part of his body.

'Don't be ridiculous!' said Blanco. 'Of course that's not me. Why would the Count want to do me any harm?'

'I don't know,' said Eva quietly. 'I just think that there's something not quite right here. I don't trust the Count. I think he's a bad man.'

'You're just imagining things,' said Blanco, beginning to get angry. He hadn't even wanted Eva to come with him to the castle and now that she was here she had no right to be criticizing everything.

'Did you believe what he said about the hole in the village?'

'Of course,' said Blanco. 'Why wouldn't I? What do you think caused it? How could the Count have had anything to do with it?'

'I just think he knew something more than he was saying at dinner,' said Eva, thinking that maybe she shouldn't have started this discussion. She had forgotten how much meeting the Count meant to Blanco and his dreams of flying. But she couldn't stop herself from continuing. 'I don't like him and I don't like this place.'

'Well, no one's asking you to stay!' said Blanco nastily. 'You shouldn't even be here in the first place. I knew I shouldn't have brought you! You've been nothing but a nuisance since I met you on that ship. I wish I had never promised your aunt that I would look after you.' He sighed in a melodramatic manner. 'But I made an oath and that means—'

'You and your stupid oath!' Eva shouted back furiously. 'That's all I've heard about since leaving the ship. I was the one who saved us remember.'

'You and your pretend angels!'

Eva narrowed her eyes at that and gave him a poisonous glare.

'You only talk about them when it suits you,' said Blanco. 'Well, I don't believe they're really there. I think your family are right—you have been touched by the moon and I can't wait to get you off my hands when we reach Barcelona! I hope your husband never lets you out of the house so that you can't annoy anyone else in the way that you annoy me!'

'*If* we reach Barcelona!' hissed back Eva. 'If your stupid, creepy old Count hasn't killed us off by then. He's evil and he doesn't really want your help. He's up to something and you just can't see past the fact that he has a flying machine! And that's a stupid idea anyway. We're not meant to fly. If we were meant to fly we would have wings already. It'll never work and you know it!'

Eva and Blanco glared furiously at each other, neither of them quite sure what to say next but both still too angry to even consider apologizing for anything that they had just said.

'Get out of here,' said Blanco eventually. 'I don't want to look at you any more.'

'But what about the letters?'

'Never mind,' he said coldly. 'I've decided that we don't need them any more. They're not important.'

Chapter 9

Days passed at the castle. Blanco would get up each morning and head off to the tower room with the Count, still furious with Eva and refusing to speak to her. He could maybe have forgiven her for what she said about the Count but insinuating that he could never hope to fly was one insult too many. Eva, in her turn, was making no effort to speak to him. How dare he say that her angels were imaginary?

For the first couple of days after their fight Eva had just slept—weeks of sleeping under the stars had left her tired and she was more than happy to remain in bed. Griffin brought her dinner every day, saying that Blanco and the Count hadn't come down to the dining room but were eating theirs in the tower room. When asked, he said that the machine was going well. She had thought that Blanco would eventually give in but he was obviously still angry with her. Well, that was fine with her—she hadn't forgiven him either.

The third day after the fight dawned bright and glorious, with sunlight streaming in wherever it could through the narrow slits in the walls. Eva couldn't bear to stay in her bed a moment longer. She got up, dressed in her new green dress, and went on to the corridor. Little pools of sunbeams lay just below each window and Eva took great delight in skipping from one to the other.

Once in the courtyard, however, she was unsure what to do next. She could wander down to the village, she supposed, but when she got to the portcullis it was down and she couldn't find anyone around to open it. Micha and Azaz had both deserted her. In fact, thinking about it, she hadn't really spoken to Azaz since they had come to the castle—he was acting very strangely—and even Micha made only sporadic appearances. So she couldn't speak to them. She took a deep breath. That left only Godoffel and Griffin and the happy smiling man whom she hadn't seen since the dinner on the first night. If she could find him then maybe she would have someone to talk to.

Rameel was more worried than he had let on. He had suspected that the lights around Eva's head may have been angels and he had warned the Count accordingly. But neither the pirate attack, the wolf, nor the pilgrims had been successful in separating Eva from Blanco and Rameel was beginning to see why. Azaz and Micha may not have known that he was in the castle but they had obviously always been determined to come here.

He still seethed with the jealousy that had caused him to fall in the first place, although it had subsided a little. It was amazing what a few aeons in the pit could do. But he still thought that he had the right to interfere with how the humans did things. What was the harm in 'helping' them to discover new ways to destroy themselves? That was their decision, after all.

Rameel enjoyed working with Count Maleficio. Even though the Count did not know the ultimate plan he had enough of a manipulative mind to want to play with all sorts of things that he shouldn't. And he did love experimenting. Rameel had been searching for a mind such as this since his release. He no longer had the powers that he once had and needed to operate through a human, but in the Count he had found the right person. Or one of the right people. Rameel did not like to limit his options. The Count was not his only friend.

She heard him before she saw him. His hood was down and she was able to see his long straggling hair which hugged his shoulders which were in turn heaving with sobs. Eva didn't think she had ever heard anything so piteous in all her life. He was sitting on one of the turrets with his legs hanging over the side. It was the side facing the path which led up to the castle and so Eva didn't think that he was planning to jump off. If he had really wanted to harm himself he would have jumped from the tower.

'Griffin?' She approached him hesitantly none-theless. He could still do some nasty damage if he jumped from there.

He started and turned in surprise and Eva had a glimpse of his face before he quickly pulled his hood up again to hide it.

'Griffin,' she said, hurrying over to him. 'Oh, Griffin, what happened to your poor face?' She pulled his hood back off and Griffin hung his head down in embarrassment. It was all red and shiny and he had no eyebrows. His hair also started halfway back along his head, as though the front piece had been torn off.

He mumbled something and pulled his hood back up. Eva sat beside him on the turret. 'I don't mind if you don't want to talk about it,' she said. 'We can talk about something else.'

Griffin wasn't sure how to respond to this. Nobody ever wanted to talk to him. Order him about, yes; hit him, yes; use him as an experiment, yes; but just to talk to him? That had never happened to him before. He didn't know what to say.

That didn't matter. Once Eva started talking there was usually no stopping her.

Blanco, meanwhile, was having great fun working on the flying machine. He had his sleeves rolled up, his hair tied back, and he was covered in dirt. The machine he was working on now had its genesis from one that the Count had worked on the previous year—one that he had tried out and had not managed to land properly because, as he had told Blanco on the day of his arrival, it did not have a tail. It was quite a large machine, much larger than any that Blanco had tried to build in Venice, although it followed many of the same principles.

It took the form of two large wings, each split into six sections, separated by thin slats of wood (a particular type of light wood called kopak that the Count had travelled to Africa for). The sections in between were made of a heavy cloth which had been stiffened with a special mixture to make it stretch tightly and firmly across the wooden slats. The outside of the cloth was thickly covered with feathers, for both the Count and Blanco believed that feathers had a magical quality which enabled birds to fly and so it made sense to cover the flying machine with them. So far the machine was very similar to the Count's previous flyer which lay in the corner, but Blanco was going to try to attach a new addition that day. The light wood, Blanco had realized early on, really made all the difference.

'My servants scoured through France and Spain and even up to Prussia, though there are only heavy woods there. But then one day I had a visit from a distinguished scholar from Cordoba and he told me of this very light wood which had been brought from Africa. I knew that to get the lightest wood possible was of the utmost importance for one must be able to float about the sky,' the Count had explained the day before.

Blanco was still feeling guilty about rifling through the Count's things and so he was planning on working extra hard that day. There were some things about the Count's design that he considered unnecessary but he thought it impolite to say. Why, for example, the large compartment behind where the pilot stood?

'Have you always wanted to fly?' he asked the Count as he laboured over a tricky edge on a piece of wood.

The Count was sitting at his table, poring over some designs. 'I?' said the Count in surprise, looking up. 'I don't want to fly. I just want to build a flying machine.'

'Oh,' said Blanco. 'I thought you wanted to fly.'

'No, my dear boy,' he said with a chuckle. 'That pleasure can be all yours when the time comes.'

Blanco flushed with delight. He had not thought he would have the chance. Maybe once the Count had successfully completed the flight himself, he had hoped for a chance but to be the one to fly it for the first time was more than he could ever have dared hope. He started to stumble out his thanks to the Count.

'But that is why I asked you to come,' said the Count. 'Why else did you think?'

Blanco was flummoxed. He had thought it was because he could build a flying machine but he saw now that so could the Count. But why would he not want to fly himself? Blanco didn't waste much time worrying over that but instead smiled to himself. He was going to be allowed to fly. His happy thoughts were tainted by memories of what he had to do for Gump. Maybe he should try a more straightforward approach to finding the letters.

'Count Maleficio,' he began, 'when you visited us in Venice . . . '

'Ah, yes,' interrupted the Count. 'I have such happy memories of that time. How is your delightful sister?'

Blanco never thought of Angelica as delightful and so it took a moment before he realized that it was she whom the Count meant.

'Well,' he said abruptly. 'Very well.'

'Betrothed yet?'

Blanco couldn't imagine any man wanting to marry his sister but he had heard many say that she was very beautiful so he supposed it might happen one day.

'No,' he said. He decided to change the subject. 'My great-uncle sends his regards.'

'Ah, yes,' said Count Maleficio, 'the intrepid explorer. Has he travelled anywhere lately?'

'No.' Blanco laughed. 'He says he can't face it since his time in prison. And I think he likes his honeyed wafers and pickled quinces too much to go away again.'

He glanced over to see if the Count reacted to the pickled quinces—Gump had created quite a scene when they had been knocked over—but the Count did not react.

'No,' continued Blanco, 'he is spending most of his time now sorting out all his correspondence, collecting together all his letters and things. I think he might write another book.'

Again he looked over at the Count and again he saw no change there. If the Count had the letters and felt in any way guilty about it then he was doing a good job of hiding his emotions. Blanco sighed. Either he was going to have to let Gump down (and Gump had been very certain that the Count had the letters) or he was going to have to try to find them.

When Griffin leapt up, saying that he had to get back to work, Eva stayed where she was, legs swinging over the battlements, enjoying the view. Having been brought up in a city, she had rarely seen so much countryside and being so high up on the cliff meant that there was a spectacular view.

'It is amazing, isn't it?' boomed a cheerful voice behind her. Eva almost fell off her perch but a strong hand gripped her upper arm and held her still. She turned and saw the happy smiling man behind her. She smiled back, glad to have some more company.

'I haven't seen you around for a few days!' he said, settling himself down beside her. 'What have you been doing?'

'Oh, sleeping mostly,' replied Eva. 'I was so tired. We've been travelling for weeks, you know.'

'It all sounds great fun,' he said. He sighed deeply. 'I wish I had travelled more when I was young.'

'You're travelling now,' said Eva. 'Didn't the Count say that you had come from the south?'

The man nodded.

'Do you mind if I ask,' said Eva hesitantly. 'How long have you known Count Maleficio?'

'Oh, only for about a year or so,' he said. He leaned over so that he could whisper directly into Eva's ear—she could feel his beard tickling her neck. 'Between you and me,' he said. 'I find him a little strange.'

'Oh, I'm so glad you said that,' said Eva, releasing a deep sigh of relief. 'So do I!'

The man laughed out loud. It was a refreshing sound in the gloomy castle and, after a moment, Eva joined in. She laughed until her sides ached, only just realizing how unhappy she had been. It was as she was gasping for a breath in between laughter that she realized that the man beside her had stopped laughing and was staring at her with his dark blue eyes.

'What?' she managed to gasp out.

'My dear,' he said, placing a gentle hand on her arm. 'I say this only out of the greatest concern for you. You must leave this place. I think the Count is a bad man and means to do you and your friend harm.'

'I knew it!' said Eva triumphantly. 'I tried to tell Blanco but he wouldn't listen.'

'Maybe you should leave alone,' he said insistently.

'I couldn't leave Blanco,' she said. 'We may not be talking now but I couldn't just leave him here.'

The man rose and smiled down at Eva. 'I'm sure I'm exaggerating things,' he said. 'The Count is just a little eccentric. I'm sure he doesn't really mean any harm.' But his anxious look belied his words and left Eva feeling very uncomfortable in the pit of her stomach.

The man smiled again.

'If you ever need any help, my dear,' he said, 'be assured you can call on me.'

'Oh, thank you!' said Eva. It made such a difference knowing that someone was on her side. The man patted her on the head and walked away.

'There's something funny going on here,' said Eva. 'Griffin's eyebrows and hair have all been burnt off and he's terrified of the Count. I don't like him myself and I wish Blanco wasn't so involved in this flying machine. Azaz isn't talking to me for some reason and neither is Blanco. What do you think, Micha?'

'*I think you shouldn't meddle too much*,' replied *Micha*.

'Do you know what's going on?' asked Eva.

She was sitting cross-legged on her bed, letting the material of the beautiful dress that the Count had given her run through her fingers. She was thinking back to her conversation with Griffin, although conversation was perhaps a generous word to use since she had done most of the talking. He had been very nervous and wouldn't tell her about how he had lost his eyebrows. He had kept scratching them, like a dog worrying at a bone, and had confessed that they were terribly itchy. Eva had suggested that he rub in some aloe vera which would ease the itching and he had looked at her gratefully. He hadn't wanted to talk about the Count's experiments or about the flying machine. In fact, he hadn't really wanted to talk at all but he had seemed happy to have her company and to listen to her chattering about the journey that she and Blanco had made. In the middle of a tale about Clara he had suddenly jumped up as though a giant hand had prodded him to attention and had insisted that he had to go and had run off.

'*Why isn't Blanco talking to you?*' asked Micha. '*And I've told you before—it's not that Azaz isn't speaking to you. He's just busy on another matter at the moment.*'

Eva shrugged. 'We fought about the Count,' she said. 'And about the flying machine. And you and Azaz. He said that he didn't believe in you. It's not easy trying to explain you two, you know.'

'*I'm sorry,*' *said Micha, floating down and coming to sit on the bed and taking Eva's hand. It felt so warm and soft. Micha longed to feel her own skin again. She had enjoyed the feel of it, how warm and soft it had been. Now her skin was alabaster cool and it made her sad to touch human skin—it reminded her too much of what she had lost. She shook her head to rid herself of her memories and turned her attention back to Eva.*

'*I know it's difficult,*' *she said, stroking Eva's untidy hair.*

Eva flung herself down on the bed. 'I wish you two had never picked me. I never asked to hear your voices. And now Blanco won't talk to me.'

Micha didn't think this was the right time to say that she would never even have met Blanco had it not been for her and Azaz. Instead she stroked Eva's hair and listened to her cry.

'You must speak to Eva,' said Micha. 'She's upset. She thinks that you're not speaking to her.'

Azaz sighed with impatience. 'I don't have time for this,' he said. 'Things are moving too fast, faster than I had anticipated.'

'You're too caught up in all this experimentation,' Micha accused. 'You have no time for Eva any more. You're beginning to care about whether Blanco gets to fly a little too much.' She narrowed her eyes. 'I hope you're not helping him.'

'Of course not,' snapped Azaz. 'I know better than to interfere.'

'I hope so,' said Micha. 'We have enough problems with Rameel. I don't need you to get into trouble as well.'

'Oh, leave me be,' said Azaz.

Griffin was frightened. His master had found out about him talking to the girl and had forbidden him any further contact. But he liked the girl.

★　　★　　★

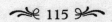

Count Maleficio stood in the doorway and looked into the room. He needed to go down to the kitchens but that meant leaving Blanco to work on the machine by himself. He wasn't yet sure if he could be trusted to be left alone in the tower room but he had little choice. He was pleased with their progress and was already thinking that the machine might be ready for flight on the morrow. He watched Blanco as he lay underneath the machine, twiddling with some of the ropes and straps. He appeared engrossed.

'Blanco!' he called and was answered with a grunt. 'I have to go somewhere for a moment. I'll be back shortly.' Blanco grunted again.

The moment the door slammed behind the Count Blanco was out from under the machine and rifling through the papers on his desk. He had had an argument constantly in his head since he had arrived at the castle and the Count had been so welcoming; but, quite apart from Gump's words echoing in his head, he also had Azaz whispering constantly in his ear.

'They're not here,' he said. 'I've looked so many times.'

'*Then they must be elsewhere. There must be a secret compartment somewhere.*'

As Blanco looked around the table, pressing knobs and whorls, Azaz looked over his shoulder at what was on the table. Blanco had been careful to move nothing out of place and the astrological chart still lay at the top of the table.

'*Blanco,*' called Azaz. '*Do you know what this is?*'

'I'm busy,' snapped Blanco. 'I can't do two things at once and the Count may not be much longer. This is the first time he's ever left me alone here.'

'*I need to show you something,*' said Azaz. '*It's important.*'

'I'm coming, I'm coming,' said Blanco. His fingers were running along the side ridge of the table as he spoke and there was a sudden loud click as his fingers slid into a hole. It was a secret catch and a drawer shot out beside him.

'Azaz!' he cried. 'There's a drawer here. And it's full of papers.'

'*Bring them out! Quickly! I can hear the Count coming.*'

Blanco, too, could hear the sound of the Count huffing and puffing as he climbed the last few stairs. Blanco had often wondered why the Count, as an inventor, had not thought of a way to get to the top of the tower without climbing the stairs. He grabbed half the papers, stuffed them down his tunic, and slammed the drawer shut before diving back underneath the flying machine.

The door creaked open a scant moment later. The Count was happy to see Blanco in the same position as he had left him. He glanced over at the table but the papers appeared undisturbed. Looking round the room he tried to catch a glimpse of the angel that Rameel had insisted was accompanying Blanco but he could see nothing. This wasn't totally surprising since he couldn't see Rameel either.

'Is it ready?' he asked Blanco.

Blanco suddenly realized that if he stood up the papers would crackle and so he remained where he was.

'Not quite,' he shouted cheerily. 'I'm having problems connecting two bits together. It's a bit fiddly.'

'I could come down and help you?' offered the Count.

'No, no,' said Blanco quickly. 'I can manage it. It just may take a while.'

The Count was quite relieved about this as he didn't really want to get down on the floor—his cloak always seemed to get in the way and he did so hate to get it dirty.

Instead he looked around the room, only just managing to restrain himself from clapping his hands together with excitement. He loved his castle. He loved his room. He loved his inventions. He had always loved experimenting. Even as a small boy he had found ways of making life easier for himself by creating or building things that would ease his way. And if the odd frog or cat had been sacrificed in order to help him, well, that was just the way of all great inventors.

Count Maleficio had grown up in a cold, isolated castle in Galicia, on the westernmost point of the land mass of Spain. His mother had died giving birth to him and his father had died just after the Count had reached his majority. No one had interfered with his work or how he lived. He ran the castle as a large laboratory with only a few servants. He would have been happy there, he thought. He looked again at Blanco's feet. If only he had never gone to Malta. He shook his head to dislodge it of thoughts of Magdalena. He did not wish to think of her for thoughts of her made him uncomfortable. Guilt was an emotion that he rarely felt but he usually felt twinges of it when he thought of Magdalena.

He looked again at Blanco's feet sticking out from

under the flying machine and a small suspicion grew. Had his great-uncle told him of their past? Did he know of Magdalena? When he had visited Venice last summer, Marco had said that he had never told any of his family anything of his adventures in Malta and Blanco had certainly never said anything about his great-uncle knowing the Count from before.

The Count was fairly certain that his past was still unknown to Blanco and he turned his attention back to his inventions. He looked over at Blanco's feet where they lay sticking out from under the machine. If only he knew what the Count really had planned for the flying machine he might not be so keen to work on it.

Blanco stretched his cramped legs.

'Have you not finished yet?' asked the Count. 'You've been under there a long time.'

Blanco had been under there a long time but this was because he was trying to find a way to get out of the room without rustling the papers.

'Just coming,' he said. The Count had sounded suspicious.

Straight-legged and keeping his upper body from moving at all, he slid himself out from under the machine and lay there. The Count looked at him.

'What are you doing?'

'Just thinking,' said Blanco. 'I do my best thinking lying down, you know.' He was wondering how he could stop the papers crackling when he stood up. He couldn't think how to move without the Count hearing them. He bit his lip.

Unwittingly, the Count saved him. Wandering over, he dropped the flying machine plans on Blanco's chest.

'You'd better study these closely tonight,' he said. 'I think you might be flying tomorrow.'

Blanco leapt to his feet, clutching the plans to his chest in gratitude for more than one reason.

Chapter 10

Blanco threw the papers out over the bed and prayed that they were the right letters. But before he looked at them properly he looked once again at the diagrams of the flying machine. He spread them out on the floor and crouched down beside them. He just could not believe that he would get to fly it tomorrow. The culmination of all his dreams, all his hopes, all finally within his reach. As he had earlier in the tower room, he pondered over the inclusion of the large compartment behind where the pilot stood. It was as though something were to be fitted in there. Turning from that puzzle, Blanco perused the machine's controls. He was slightly nervous about keeping control of it in the air. If only the wind was strong on the morrow—but not too strong—then he might have a chance of flight. The thought of the machine not working, or what would happen to him if it failed, did not even enter his head.

There was a little knock on the door. Blanco did not hear it and it came again, a little louder this time. He looked up in surprise, his eyes glazed over, so engrossed was he in his plans.

'Come in!' he called, expecting Griffin.

A small head with a tangled mess of hair looked hesitantly round the door.

'Blanco,' said Eva forlornly, 'it's me. Can I come in?'

In his excitement about getting to fly the next day, Blanco forgot that he was supposed to be annoyed with her and waved her into the room.

'What are you doing?' she asked. 'How is the flying machine? I'm sorry I was so rude about it.'

'Well,' he said, hating to apologize but knowing that he would have to, especially since he had been having long conversations with Azaz over the past few days, 'I'm sorry that I was rude about your angels. I really do believe in them.'

'Good,' said Eva. 'I hated not talking.'

'Eva!' Blanco said, looking up from the papers on the floor in delight. 'It's ready. The flying machine is finally ready.' He paused. 'I'm to fly it tomorrow.'

'You are?' said Eva in surprise. 'Why isn't the Count flying it?'

'Because he said I could,' snapped Blanco, annoyed that she couldn't just have been pleased for him without asking questions. Why did she always have to ask questions?

'Oh, Blanco,' said Eva, 'please don't let's be cross again. I couldn't bear it.' Her bottom lip began to quiver.

Blanco, like any boy his age, could not bear to see girls crying and would do anything to stop it. Also he was amazed—he had never seen anything upset Eva before. 'Oh, don't cry,' he said gruffly. 'Of course I haven't fallen out with you again. Come over here and I'll show you the plans.'

But Eva had been sidetracked by what lay on the bed.

'What are these?' she asked, spotting the sheets of paper that Blanco had thrown carelessly down there. She picked one up and started to look at it. It made little sense and she turned it round. Still it meant nothing to her.

'Those are Gump's letters,' said Blanco, getting to his feet and coming to join her. 'At least I think they are. I found them in a secret compartment in the Count's desk.'

'Blanco,' began Eva hesitantly. She really didn't want to fall out with him again. 'What do you think of the Count?'

'I think he's a genius,' said Blanco, not giving her question his full attention—that was caught by the plans he was looking at. These were not Gump's letters but they were certainly something interesting. 'Some of his inventions are amazing. I don't know where he gets his ideas from. Do you know he has . . . what *is* this?'

'I think there's something strange going on here,' said Eva. 'Griffin won't talk about any of the Count's experiments or about anything. And that man at dinner said—'

'Maybe Griffin's just loyal,' interrupted Blanco, turning the plan round.

'Or he's just plain terrified,' said Eva. 'Blanco, do you know why the Count is building a flying machine?'

Blanco took his attention away from the plan for a second. 'I'll admit there is something unusual there,' he said. 'I assumed that he was building one because he wanted to fly it. That's why I build them. And everyone else who builds them does it for the same reason, I would have thought. But he said tonight that he didn't want to fly it. That's why I'm allowed to.' Blanco smiled. 'Although I'm not complaining about that.'

'But Azaz and Micha . . . ' began Eva.

'Oh,' said Blanco, turning his attention to the plan again. 'There something I've been meaning to tell you about Azaz. *Wait a moment . . . what?*'

He looked closer at the plans and then held them away from his face again as if in disbelief. He muttered something to himself and then placed them on the bed, tracing along parts of them, as though following an experiment to its logical conclusion.

'I don't think we should be doing this,' hissed Micha. *'We should have just warned Eva about Rameel.'*

'We don't have any other choice,' said Azaz. *'Help me or go away.'*

Micha concentrated. 'He's definitely down here,' she said finally.

'If only these humans knew what few powers we had,' said Azaz, *'they wouldn't revere us so much.'*

'We used to have more,' said Micha mournfully. *'Raphael and Gabriel and the others still have theirs.'*

'Ah, but what use are they, now they're not allowed on to Earth?' asked Azaz.

'That was our fault.'

'And we're still paying the price,' said Azaz. *'But unless you want to pay a bigger one, you'll help me find Rameel and stop him doing what he's planning on doing.'*

'I'm still not exactly sure what that is,' said Micha.

'Remember when we fell,' said Azaz.

'Of course,' said Micha, nodding her golden head emphatically, her eyes filled with sadness. *'As if I could ever forget!'*

'You fell for love,' said Azaz. 'I fell because I wanted to interfere. I wanted to teach humans about science and art and magic, about how to use their brains to explore the world around them. About how they didn't have to rely on the Creator to invent everything but how they could create some things for themselves too. I suppose I thought I could do a better job.' His eyes flashed slightly as though, in some ways, he still thought that he could. 'We were wrong and we took our punishment.' He saw Micha open her mouth to protest and he forestalled her. 'You were wrong, Micha, even if for the right reason. You were not supposed to fall in love with a human.'

Micha looked slightly mutinous but nodded. Her punishment had been to lose her wings, to live the span of a human life on earth, loving her human, and then to have her wings returned and to live forever mourning the loss of her love.

'Rameel fell for much the same reason as me,' Azaz continued. 'But our outlooks were different. I wanted to teach humans the beauty of new things, how they could improve their existence. Rameel wanted only to destroy them because he was jealous of them. He didn't want to bow to God's creation because he thought he was superior to them. He didn't like the way that God loved them. He was like a spoilt child. It's the same with these humans. They want the same things but for different reasons. Blanco wants to fly because he thinks it will be beautiful. He wants to know what it feels like to be a bird. The Count, on the other hand—'

'Are you looking for me?' a silken voice came from behind them.

Rameel was not alone. The short, round, merry-looking man from dinner was standing beside him. He was dwarfed by the giant angel whose long, gleaming black hair reached down to the head of his companion. The little man was beaming, looking happy to be there, as if he had been invited to a party.

'Can you see them?' Rameel asked him.

'No,' said the man, in a mellifluous voice sounding disappointed, although he still smiled benignly upon them all. His rosy cheeks were smooth and his eyes were hidden between the apples of his cheeks and his bushy white eyebrows.

'You will just have to trust me then,' said Rameel smoothly, his murky eyes gleaming in the angels' direction. 'Directly in front of us is Azaz, the one-time leader of the rebel angels. By his side is the beautiful Micha, who fell, not through rebellion, but through love for a human.' His tone made it clear what he thought of Micha's actions.

'At least I loved once,' spat out Micha. 'That is something you'll never know, Rameel, for you love only yourself.'

'That is not true,' said Rameel, 'for I love power almost as much.' He threw back his head and laughed at that.

'I stand corrected,' said Micha stiffly.

'You must love that pit you were in,' interrupted Azaz, 'because that is where you will be returning.'

Rameel flinched slightly at that. The torments of the pit were still too fresh in his mind for him to discard that threat entirely. He had spent longer there than the others for he had not repented. 'Not this time,' he said.

'What's happening?' asked the Stranger. 'What are they saying?'

'Nothing of interest,' said Rameel. 'Come, let us go.'

'Oh no,' said Azaz, standing in front of Rameel. He topped him by an inch. 'Not till you tell me what you're doing.'

The air filled with turbulence. The wings of all three angels were pulsating. Sparks flew from them: Rameel's were dark indigo blue, Micha's a vibrant yellow-gold, and Azaz's crimson red. The Stranger stared openmouthed. He could not remain unaffected by the change of energy in the room.

Azaz was determined that Rameel should not leave that room. Rameel was equally determined that he should. They faced each other, each waiting for the other to strike the first blow. In the event it was Rameel who did so, fuelled not so much by his wish to leave as by his hatred of Azaz. His large wing struck Azaz across the face, instantly raising an angry weal. Azaz snarled and raised his own wings in anger. In an instant, they were entangled and the fight was in full flow.

It wasn't until this moment that Micha realized that the Stranger had gone.

'Well, these certainly aren't Gump's letters,' said Blanco, placing them on the bed again and stepping back slightly. 'But they are very interesting nonetheless.'

'What are they?' asked Eva, coming to stand beside him and putting her plans on the bed beside his.

'More plans,' said Blanco. 'But not for flying machines. And I don't think for anything good. Look!' He pointed to a castle standing and then to it in ruins. The same thing again for a walled town. In both instances there was a middle diagram showing flames and with the entire building being thrown up into the air.

'I don't understand,' said Eva. 'What is causing the buildings to be destroyed?'

'I'm not sure,' said Blanco, 'but I think it's something to do with these ingredients here.' He pointed to diagrams of a basket of charcoal, a container of sulphur, and something else which looked like a rotting log. 'I'm sure that I've seen something like this in plans that my great-uncle brought back from the court of the Great Khan.' He bit his lip, trying to make sense of it all. 'In fact, these may even be the plans that my great-uncle brought back. They look terribly familiar.'

'Blanco,' said Eva, still looking at her own plan. 'I think this is a map of the village and, look.' She pointed at one building in the middle. It was a church. 'There wasn't a church in the village when we came in. I've only just realized it.'

'No,' agreed Blanco, 'but there is a hole the size of a church.'

They stared at each other in fear and amazement. What could possibly be powerful enough to destroy a church? And did they really want to find out?

'What shall we do, Blanco?' whispered Eva. It suddenly seemed right to whisper. Things were happening here that made her afraid. And where were Azaz and Micha?

Blanco wasn't sure what to say. He had not expected this. He had been looking for Gump's love letters, not for these. The Count was interested in all sorts of experimentation but surely only because he was an inventor. Looking at these different plans laid out on his bed, Blanco was no longer so sure that was the only reason.

Gathering up the plans he stuck them back down his tunic. Eva was watching him, her green eyes large with fright but also with complete faith that he knew what he was doing.

'I'm going to find Gump's letters and put these back,' he said confidently. 'And then I'll come back and we can discuss what we're going to do. Will you stay here?'

Eva wasn't sure. She felt as though she had been ducked in a cold bath but Blanco was looking at her impatiently. She nodded and he left.

Chapter 11

The Count was in a little room off the tower room when he turned to find the Stranger standing behind him.

'The angels are fighting,' the Stranger said, smiling in enjoyment. 'That should keep them out of our way for a while.'

He sat down in one of the chairs next to the fire and stretched out his feet to the flames. He looked round the tiny room. It was lined with books and bottles. The books were all beautifully bound in leather and had long titles such as *How to Change Shape or Become Invisible in Ten Easy Steps*. Many of the bottles contained beautifully coloured liquids, ranging across the whole spectrum from ruby red to an almost translucent blue. The Stranger smiled. The colours reminded him of the angels fighting. Some of the other bottles were not so pleasant. They contained dried up bats, the paws of innumerable animals, wings, toenails, skin, and other things that caused the Stranger to shudder in disgust.

'I don't know how you can bear to look at these things, Maleficio, never mind use them,' he said.

The Count looked up from his table where he was scribbling on a sheet of paper. 'You don't complain when they work,' he said impatiently. 'How else do you think I can do half the things I do?'

The Stranger shrugged his shoulders. He was no longer smiling and his face looked strained in repose. If he didn't smile his cheeks looked too big for his face. Relaxed like this, his lips were small and petty. He watched the Count writing up his reports from the day. He knew that was what he was doing because he knew the Count was a creature of habit and that he was careful to write up all that had happened with his experiments each day.

Count Maleficio was indeed writing up an account of what Blanco had been doing with the flying machine but he was also watching the Stranger. Although he had known him for a number of years he did not fully trust him and was not entirely sure what he was doing here. He was one of a band of inventors whom the Count had met in southern Spain, in the city of Cordoba. Most had been students of alchemy seeking eternal life, immense wealth or, in most cases, both. But there were also many experimenters and Maleficio had been in communication with a few of them about the flying machine. He had gone to Cordoba to meet them and one of the people he had been introduced to was the Stranger. He was experimenting with Greek fire and other explosive ideas and he had taken the Count under his wing. The group he belonged to was full of grand plans and each of them brought something to it. The Stranger led them. Maleficio knew that he had a plan for all of their experiments but he hadn't told any of them what the plan was yet. The Count, though he barely liked to admit it to himself, was sometimes a little scared of the Stranger.

'How is the boy shaping up?' the Stranger asked abruptly.

'Excellently,' said the Count, instantly forgetting his thoughts about the Stranger, so delighted was he with the thought of seeing the fruition of his own plans. 'He has finished the flying machine and will fly it tomorrow at dawn.'

'Will it work?'

The Count looked insulted by this. 'Of course,' he said and then he modified his answer a little. 'Well, it should.' He shrugged. 'If it doesn't, at least it won't be me who's killed. I can always try again later. But it will work. Rameel has promised me.'

'Lucky you met the boy in Venice,' said the Stranger.

The Count snorted. 'It was not luck. Rameel directed me to him. And it was a pleasure to thwart his great-uncle. If it hadn't been for those plans of his that I stole we would never have tried to experiment with the fire-powder. That combined with the flying machines will bring us great rewards.'

The Stranger frowned. 'Personal battles should never have been brought into it. And Rameel shouldn't be used to further your personal vendettas.' He paused. The Count said nothing but looked furious. 'I would lay more trust in the fire-powder than the flying machines,' he continued in a more placating tone. 'If they do to a city's walls in a large amount what they did to Griffin's hair when we lit such a small amount then how can anyone refuse us anything? And look what happened to the church.' He paused. 'If the flying machine works tomorrow and the boy survives what will you do with him then?'

The Count was unsure exactly what answer the Stranger was expecting and so he hesitated before he replied. 'Kill him?' he said, a slight question in his voice, as though checking it was the correct response. 'Him and that girl he brought with him.'

'Good,' replied the Stranger coolly. 'I don't know why you didn't kill the girl as soon as she arrived.'

'She did have some angelic assistance,' replied the Count drily.

The Stranger waved his hand. 'Rameel will take care of that.'

There was a loud, resonant crash from outside the door.

'What was that?'

Eva was sitting on the windowsill in Blanco's room counting all the stars that she could see from his window. It was boring work but it was all she could think of to do to pass the time until he returned. It took her a while to realize that she was not alone in the room.

Griffin knew that he shouldn't be there. But he knew his master was in the tower room and he knew the demon angel was still fighting and he thought he would be safe for a while. This didn't stop his hands from shaking and his heart from thudding so hard within his skin that he thought it might burst out. But he liked the girl. She had been kind to him.

'Who's there?' demanded Eva.

A scuffling in the fireplace was followed by one ragged foot and then another one. Eva recognized them at once and ran over to help him out of the fireplace.

'Griffin!' she cried. 'What are you doing here?'

Griffin's mouth was so dry with terror at the thought of defying his master that he couldn't speak at first. If he were caught . . . but he couldn't think any more about that or he would never be able to say anything.

'You must leave here,' he whispered in his hoarse voice, so low that Eva had to strain to hear him. 'You must go now.'

'We can't,' said Eva. 'Blanco won't leave now. He is going to fly the machine tomorrow. He'll never leave before he gets a chance to do that.'

'Even if *your* life is in danger?'

This silenced Eva for a moment. She didn't know how to reply to that. Would Blanco choose her over the chance to fly that machine? She suddenly realized that she wasn't sure. She knew how much he wanted to fly, how obsessed he was with the idea of flying, how it had filled his every waking—and probably sleeping—moment since he had been here but she had no idea how he felt about her.

'The Count is not working alone,' said Griffin. 'He has a dark angel.'

Eva's face brightened at the word 'angel'. 'I have two of them,' she said happily. 'I'm sure they could fight a dark one and win.'

Griffin looked surprised, so far as a man with no eyebrows or lashes could look any more surprised. 'Do you have to brew that horrid potion?' he asked.

'Potion?' laughed Eva. 'No. I just speak to them.'

Griffin looked even more miserable than usual. 'You are lucky,' he said mournfully. 'I have to brew a horrid potion to call the angel and then he stays for a few days before he disappears again. He's here now.'

Eva looked thoughtful. So that was what Micha and Azaz had been doing for the last few days.

'There is something else,' said Griffin, looking around the room, as though expecting Blanco to leap out from under the bed. 'Where is your friend? I should tell you both together.'

'He's gone to the tower room,' said Eva. She hesitated and then realized that Griffin was risking a lot coming to warn them and so she continued, 'We found some plans, something to do with flames and buildings falling down. Blanco had been looking for something that he thought the Count had taken from his great-uncle but he found them instead. He's gone to put them back.'

Griffin had pushed his hood back from his head as she spoke and was scratching at his missing eyelashes in terror.

'Not the fire-powder,' he said. 'Not the plans with the fire-powder. If my master finds them gone, he will kill him. Now. This instant.'

'But the Count likes him,' said Eva. 'He wants him to fly the machine. He won't kill him.'

Griffin stared at her. His muddy brown eyes were straining in their eye sockets as he tried to speak through his terror. 'The Count is not my master,' he said.

Scared by what she saw in his eyes Eva ran out of the door.

Blanco couldn't believe that he had knocked over the astrolabe. Of all the things to have knocked over that was certainly the heaviest and therefore the loudest. The crash resonated in his ears as he tried to decide in an instant whether he should hide or whether he should tell them that he had come back to work on the flying machine. The chilling words about his and Eva's death certainly made him prefer the former option but would he have the time?

It would appear not. The dark wall hanging on the far side of the room was thrust aside and the Count came storming through, his silver cloak billowing out behind him like an angry cloud. Just behind him came the small round man from dinner with a delighted smile on his face. Looking at him and his twinkling eyes, Blanco began to wonder if he hadn't dreamt the whole conversation that he had just listened to. This man reminded him of the old men who sat in the piazzas at home and talked of how much better things had been in their young days.

'What are you doing here?' demanded the Count.

'I . . . I . . . ' Blanco was too well aware of the fire-powder plans in his tunic to lie confidently. Eventually he managed to control his tongue which had tried to twist away from him. 'I just came to check on the flying machine. I was too excited, could not sleep.'

The Count frowned, unconvinced. Blanco was looking awkward. But then, he was obsessed with that machine and maybe what he said was true. And he wanted to see the machine fly. If they killed him now he might never know if it worked. He turned to the Stranger.

'Rameel will know if he speaks the truth,' he said. 'Where is he? I would have thought that he would be back here by now.'

Blanco looked from the Count to the small man. The Count sounded almost deferential. And who was Rameel?

'*Tell him that Rameel won't be back for a while,*'

said a voice in Blanco's ear. He recognized it as belonging to Azaz. '*Tell him . . .*'

But before Blanco had a chance to, the door to the tower room was thrown open and a heavily puffed Eva stood there. When she saw Blanco she ran over to him and threw her arms around him. She was still unable to speak, breathing too heavily. Azaz continued speaking into Blanco's ear.

'*What are you saying?*' asked a voice.

'*Isn't it a shame,*' asked Azaz, turning cold eyes on Rameel, '*that your friends have to burn some concoctions to be able to hear you and Blanco and Eva can hear us without even trying.*'

'Get off me!' cried Blanco, taking Eva's arm from around his neck. He looked embarrassed. 'What are you doing?'

Eva glared at the Count and then smiled at the man standing beside him, the man who had been so kind to her at dinner. 'Señor . . . ' She hesitated, suddenly realizing that she still didn't know his name. 'Señor, you must help us. The Count . . . '

'I told you not to trust him,' said the man, smiling at her, this time in a pitying manner.

'I know,' said Eva while Count Maleficio threw him a murderous glare.

'Then you should have listened,' said the man, his smile beginning to fade. 'I told you to leave the castle.'

'I know,' said Eva, glancing at Blanco. 'But I couldn't leave—'

'Oh, not this again. Not more declarations about how you couldn't leave your little friend,' interrupted the Stranger, smiling at Eva. 'It's all too tedious for words. He would have left you fast enough if it had been the choice between you and flying, you know.'

'No, he wouldn't!' cried Eva and then she looked at Blanco. He was staring not at her but at the flying machine. He tore his gaze away as she spoke.

'I . . . I—' he said.

'I've had enough,' interrupted the Stranger and then he turned away. 'Kill them.'

All three of them looked at him with horror.

'No!' cried the Count. 'He's got to fly first.'

'No!' cried Blanco, who quite agreed with the Count. If he was going to die, he was going to do it while trying to fly.

'No!' cried Eva looking in shock at the man she had thought her friend.

He smiled at her again. 'You shouldn't have trusted me either, my dear,' he said. 'You really are just too trusting. It looks as if we've all let you down.' He motioned to himself, Count Maleficio, and Blanco.

'*Not all of us!*' cried Azaz, heading towards the Stranger. Just as he was about to reach him, a hand grasped his wing, twisting it viciously. Crying out in pain he turned to see Rameel.

The Stranger turned cold eyes on the angels and Eva realized that he could see them. But that he could do so he was keeping secret from the Count and also, she thought, from the angels.

Eva gasped in horror. This must be the dark angel

that Griffin had mentioned. Rameel's wings were torn and his left one was hanging heavily from his shoulder blade. The blood, where it ran out, was of a metallic silvery colour and where it dripped on to the floor it sizzled and dissolved instantly. He was limping and he cradled his left arm carefully against his side as though it hurt dreadfully. But he had hold of Azaz with his one good hand and he was pulling at Azaz's wing. Azaz turned round in a rage and pulled at Rameel's hand. Their eyes were blazing in anger and their faces twisted in hatred. Azaz grabbed Rameel's left hand, causing him to howl in anguish but he refused to let go.

Their moves were almost too quick for Eva to see but whatever they were doing it looked painful. Before her horrified eyes, they fought their way over to the windowsill. Azaz jumped on to the sill to give himself greater leverage to fight off Rameel but Rameel with one last burst of energy lunged forward and pushed Azaz backwards. Azaz, recovering from a previous attack, was off balance and stumbled. A smile of triumph flickered momentarily over Rameel's face before Azaz reached out a hand and grasped the trailing edge of Rameel's wing. When Azaz disappeared over the ledge Rameel followed him howling curses as he fell.

As they had been fighting the rest had stood still, as though turned to statues. The angels had fought in a terrifying silence echoed by the humans in the room. As soon as they disappeared over the edge, however, everybody came back as though waking from a dream.

'There's one thing I want to know before you kill us,' said Eva turning to the Count, calmly as though discussing what she would like to have for dinner. 'Why did you need Blanco in the first place? Why didn't you just try to fly yourself?'

'My dear girl,' said the Count in tones of outrage. 'I might have hurt myself. *You* must understand what I mean, Blanco,' he continued coldly, turning away from Eva. 'Great experiments demand sacrifices. Someone has to make them. It is an honour for you to take part in my experiments.'

'You are supposed to make sacrifices *yourself*,' Blanco said. 'Not turn other people into them. I don't understand you. I want to make a flying machine. But *I* want to fly. I want to feel what it is like. Don't you understand that? Don't you want to try that yourself?'

Count Maleficio stared at Blanco as though he were lacking in his wits and then he grabbed his arm and pulled him over to the ledge where the flying machine lay. Looking past it Blanco could see little for it was still dark, although far off in the distance dawn was struggling to break through. It was a windy night and the clouds were forcing it to fight hard to be seen.

'Do you have any idea,' he hissed in Blanco's ear, 'just how high up we are here?'

Blanco nodded. 'Of course I do,' he said. 'It's wonderful!'

He had looked out often in the past few days while working on the machine and had thought it was wonderful how high the castle was. The chance of a successful flight was so much greater leaping from here. The Count ignored his nod, however.

'The tower is the height of the cliff that the castle rests upon. I did my calculations to find the highest tower possible on top of the highest cliff that I could find inland to give my machines the greatest chance of success. To give *me* the greatest chance of success.' His fingers were gripping Blanco's arm so tightly now that it was painful. '*I* did the calculations, *I* created the designs, but I needed someone to test them for me for I could not bear to even look out.' He paused and then turned Blanco to him, gazing into his eyes as though defying him to laugh. 'I cannot bear to look out,' he said. 'I find I do not like the height.'

Eva bit back a nervous giggle. It did seem strange, a man so obsessed with flying who was afraid of heights. That must have been why he recreated the stars inside—so that he did not have to look out to see them.

'That is why I now have need of you,' he said, still gripping on to Blanco's arm. 'I need someone who knows what he is doing to see if the machine will truly work. I need to know if my machine can really fly.' His strange glittering eyes were looking straight into Blanco's. 'Then I can build more. Hundreds! Thousands!'

Blanco suddenly realized what the compartment was for. It was for the fire-powder. If they could light the fire-powder and release it from above a walled town then they would indeed be invincible. Nobody could fight back against an attack from the skies. They must never find out that Blanco had the plans for the fire-powder. He had to leave the castle with them and hope that they had not copied them.

The Count released Blanco's arm and pushed him back towards the far wall. He turned and looked out at the slowly lightening sky and then turned back to face them all, his cloak whirling around him. He was laughing. He raised his arms as though calling to the heavens.

'I have a vision!' he cried. 'Imagine the sky filled with men in flying machines.'

Blanco at least could share that vision. It could be a beautiful thing. It was what he longed for. But what Count Maleficio said next shattered those illusions.

'Like great black bats they will fill the skies, casting their shadow upon the earth. And they will be filled with poison or fire or missiles. Venom will pour from them on to the people below. They will destroy whole villages in moments. Towns in half a day. Castles will fall! Nobody will be able to stop them. Nobody will know how to prevent them or to fight against them! Except me!' His voice rose. 'Me! I will have their power in my hands. They will do what I say. *Everyone* will do as I say!'

He paused and his strange grey eyes focused for a moment on Blanco and he spoke to him as though sharing a great secret. 'At first I thought of how much kings would pay me to build such things. They would be helpless against them. How do you protect your castle from a threat from above? You cannot. Do you have any idea how many kings would pay to own such a weapon?'

Blanco and Eva shook their heads in dumbfounded horror at what he was saying. He continued as though one of them had actually answered him.

'And then I thought, wait! Why should they pay me for my machines? I can have my own power. I can threaten everyone. There is no one who can stop me. So why can I not be a king? Why can I not rule the earth? With these machines at my bidding, nothing and no one can stop me! I *can* rule the world!'

He stood there, his eyes glittering in triumph as he contemplated his dreams of mass destruction, his arms still raised to some unknown demon of flight that held his soul in thrall.

'Really, Maleficio,' said the Stranger. All three turned to him in surprise having forgotten that he was still there. 'You do like to dramatize things, don't you?'

His smile had never wavered but his eyes had grown hard. He did not like what he had just heard.

Blanco was horrified and barely heard what the Stranger said. To him, flight had always been like a gift from heaven. He had always thought of it as being a beautiful, graceful thing. He had always thought of birds when he thought of flying. Not this, not death and destruction and visions of terror. The Count had ruined all his dreams, all his hopes. Now he would never be able to look at another flying machine without thinking of the terrible things they could be used for.

'No!' he shouted, trying to stop the Count from speaking further. 'I won't let you! I will smash the machine first!'

'Will you, Blanco?' said the Count, quieter now, staring into his eyes, his own bright with a lust for power. He shrugged his shoulders. 'Would you not like to build them with me? I could let you have a town or two. I was always planning on doing so anyway.'

Blanco picked up a metal hammer.

'Don't touch that machine, Blanco,' said the Count and then he shrugged. 'I will only build another if you smash it,' he added.

'But who will you get to fly it?' Blanco asked. 'If you are too scared of heights and I refuse to get in?'

Blanco turned to the machine. He was reluctant to smash it. It was a beautiful thing, despite what the Count wanted to use it for, and he was sure that it would work.

'I think I can say something here.'

The Count and Blanco both turned. The Stranger held Eva in his encircling arm. She was pale and her eyes were even larger than usual in her terror. At least Blanco thought it was terror. Looking again, he saw that it was anger.

'I think you *will* fly it,' said the man in his soft voice, his teeth shining through the murky half-light in the room. The sight sent shivers up and down Blanco's spine. 'Unless you want your friend to die.'

Blanco stared at him in shock and saw that he held a knife in his hand. He was such an ordinary looking man but his voice was pure evil. The blue eyes, looking into his, showed no emotion. Blanco felt that the Stranger truly did not care whether Eva lived or not.

He smiled cruelly at him. 'Get in, Blanco.'

'Smash it, Blanco,' cried Eva. 'I don't care what he does to me.'

Blanco looked from her to the Count to the man who held her. He realized that *he* cared what the Stranger did. He would have cared even if the Stranger had held Griffin in his arms but the fact that it was Eva made him care more than he could ever have imagined. There was no doubt in his mind that the man would kill her if he did not do as he said.

'Who are you?' Blanco asked the Stranger.

'Does it matter?' he replied. 'You probably won't live long enough to care. You know, I'm not sure that we do need you to fly that machine. I doubt it will work and I doubt that, if by some miracle it does, you will be able to control it.'

'I can fly that machine,' Blanco returned.

The Stranger shrugged. 'I find I don't really care,' he said. 'This was Maleficio's plan. I'm just here as a courtesy. But I have plenty of others. As for you, Maleficio.' He turned to the Count. 'Going to rule the world by yourself, were you? What about the rest of us?'

The Count looked furious and terrified at the same time. He gazed at the Stranger pleadingly. 'You all laughed at me,' he said sounding like a petulant child.

The Stranger silenced him with a quick snap of his fingers.

Blanco knew he had to make the Stranger care that he could fly the machine.

'It will do as he says,' he said, motioning towards the Count. 'If it works, you will be able to control whole towns. The Count is right. They'll be terrified.'

That sparked a small light of interest in his eyes. 'I have other plans that will work just as well,' he said again, 'but this would definitely speed things up. Go on then. Prove it.'

'I will do it,' Blanco said quietly. 'On one condition. I will fly if Eva is in the machine with me.'

The Stranger glanced at the Count, who seemed a little put out at being ignored in the negotiations. The Count nodded.

Eva appeared more terrified at this prospect than

at the thought that the Count or his friend might kill her.

'Do you think that's a good idea, Blanco?' she asked hesitantly, glancing at the fragile machine which looked as though it would barely hold one person's weight, never mind two.

Blanco ignored her. 'Put her in,' he said to the Stranger.

The Stranger looked at Blanco and then at Eva and then at the machine. Blanco realized that he now wanted to see it fly more than he wanted to kill Eva.

Ignoring Eva's protests, he dragged her over and strapped her into the back of it with ropes under instruction from the Count, whose eyes were sparkling at the thought that he might finally see his great invention take flight.

'Now you,' the Stranger said.

'You are mad,' Blanco said facing the Count. 'How can you dream of destruction with such a beautiful thing.'

'Power,' whispered the Count. 'I need power.'

Blanco went over to the machine, not looking once at Eva. He knew that if he saw her terror he would never be able to do what he was going to do.

'Now get in,' said the Count. The Stranger stepped back and crossed his arms.

'You'll have to help me prepare it first,' Blanco said.

The machine was still at the back of the ledge. It needed to be pushed forward ready for that one final push that would take it over the edge. Together they propelled it forward. Eva screamed as she saw the drop that was outside the ledge.

'Blanco!' she screamed. 'Don't leave me in here. Get me out!'

The machine was balanced precariously. One small push and it would be over. Smiling, the Count pretended to push it and Eva screamed once more.

He was now staring at Blanco, waiting for him to climb in. Blanco had walked over to the fire and when he turned the Count saw that he held something in his hand.

'What are you doing?' he demanded angrily, coming towards him. The Stranger looked on with indifference. He was curious now to see whether the machine would work.

'This,' Blanco said, turning and throwing the sticks he had in his hand into the fire.

While the Count stared open-mouthed Blanco dodged past him. The Count had rushed to the fire and was trying to remove the sticks but he was too late. Blanco could not see what the Stranger was doing.

A moment later the whole room shattered with colour.

The sticks had exploded and one caught the Count on the side of the face causing him to howl in pain. For a moment Blanco just stood and stared as the brightly coloured rockets streamed around the room, red and green and gold and silver, all shooting out from the fire. And then the rockets seemed to head straight for the window and he leapt into the flying machine, pushing it forward as he did so. The Count's shout of anger was the last thing he heard as the machine fell forward into the night sky.

Chapter 12

'Hang on!' Blanco yelled to Eva as the machine took a wild dip to the ground. 'It'll straighten out in a minute.'

At least Blanco certainly hoped so. The machine was swinging wildly in the wind and he was finding it hard to work out how high up they were given how dark it was. Having two people on it was not helping either as it was only built for one. He could feel part of the framework under his feet crack a little under the strain and could only hope that Eva couldn't feel it too.

He finally managed to gain a little height by pulling on the ropes that moved the wings while leaning back on the framework. This movement caused the front to rise a little since Eva, who was at the back, was lighter than he was.

What he couldn't see was that Micha was lifting the machine at the back. Eva couldn't see her either as she had her eyes screwed tight shut with sheer terror. But Micha knew that she couldn't hold the machine together forever. Micha had not realized how much of her strength it would take. Where was Azaz?

Blanco looked back and saw that the whole tower room was on fire. The rockets had obviously caught on all the wooden machinery that was in the room and it was now ablaze. He spared a thought for the Count and the Stranger. He wondered if they had got away.

It was at this moment that it dawned on Blanco that he was flying. All his dreams were coming true but he would never have imagined that these would have been the circumstances. There were no birds, there was no feeling of freedom, just one of fear and loathing and terror of what the future of the flying machine would be.

But then he realized that they weren't so much flying as falling, albeit in a controlled way. The height of the tower and the cliff combined meant that the woodwork caught on the wind and thus slowed their fall. Despite tugging on the ropes he was doing little to steer their course. If anything, the machine was steering them. It went with the wind and it carried them inexorably downwards.

Micha could not hold them much longer. She could slow their fall, make it appear as though they were flying, but her wings were tiring. The machine was so heavy, so cumbersome. Flying with humans was not the same as flying with angels.

In a last attempt Blanco pulled on the wing ropes. They flapped feebly. He had never been convinced that they should move. He had favoured a more rigid structure but the Count, calling on his study of birds, had been adamant that they should flap as birds'

wings did. A loud creaking greeted this motion and he watched in horror as one of the slats snapped.

Azaz appeared beside Micha and took much of the strain from her. She smiled at him. 'What took you so long?' she asked.

Azaz smiled grimly. 'Rameel,' he said. 'He took longer than I thought.'

'And has he gone?' asked Micha.

'For a while,' said Azaz sadly. 'Only for a while.' He looked at the flying machine falling to pieces in front of him and saw that Eva still had her eyes tight shut. 'Open your eyes, Eva,' he commanded.

Eva opened her eyes in time to see the ground rushing towards them. But she had heard her angels speak—both of them—and she knew that everything would be all right. So she looked ahead at the coming dawn and the beauty of seeing the world from a new perspective and she smiled.

The real test, Blanco knew, would come in the landing. That had been the problem with the previous machine. It was the tail that the Count had insisted on adding that might save their lives.

Blanco looked ahead and saw that dawn was breaking through the hills. He headed for the light spreading across the sky. The framework beneath their feet was really beginning to crack now. Bits of the machine were falling off. Blanco was standing on only one piece of wood where previously there had been six and he could hear even that begin to crack beneath his weight. The tightening of Eva's arm around his waist persuaded him that she too was standing on flimsy ground. At least she wasn't screaming. There was no option but to try to land. In the slowly spreading light he thought that he could be fairly sure that there were no trees beneath them and that they would land on flat ground.

'Eva!' he shouted and she pinched his waist to show that she had heard him. 'I'm going to try to land.'

It was time to test out the tail. Blanco leaned forward to cause most of the weight to fall in that direction. Eva screamed as the ground rushed up to meet them. Too fast. Blanco leant back quickly and the machine lifted again, but they were closer to the ground now and slowing fast. He pulled the tail to the right and then the left and the machine slowed down more and this time they approached the ground in a more measured manner. The sun was rising fast now and they could see the ground quite clearly. They were just outside the village.

'There may be a slight bump,' he shouted over his shoulder. 'Prepare yourself.'

Eva and Blanco were jolted heavily out of the machine as it landed, both of them rolling free from the framework as it cracked ominously. Blanco bit back a cry of agony as he felt his arm bend under him.

Suddenly the machine's framework, those bits of it which hadn't already broken, gave a loud creak and collapsed completely into just a pile of wood and a few forlorn bits of material to which feathers were still attached. But at least they had managed to land before its disintegration.

They stood in silence in each other's arms. It was actually quite comfortable to stand there, together, like that. Particularly after such an excitement. Blanco could feel Eva's breath in his ear where her cheek rested on his shoulder and his good arm tightened around her. He could not believe they were both still alive.

'I flew,' Blanco said quietly. 'I really flew.'

The angels said nothing but they looked at each other and smiled.

'You did it,' acknowledged Eva. 'You did what you set out to do.'

Blanco was happy that she was so pleased for him and so he was all the more shocked when she stepped back and then kicked him hard in the shins.

'Ow!' he cried. 'What was that for?'

'For putting me in that machine,' she said furiously. 'I have never been so terrified in my whole life!'

'Well, if that's all the thanks I get for saving your life . . . ' he began huffily, but stopped when she reached out and caught hold of his hand.

'Ow!' Blanco cried again, this time in genuine pain for his arm was really aching now.

'What is it?' she cried. 'Are you hurt? You should sit down.'

'Close your eyes.'

As soon as he did, he was filled by a warm glowing sensation, much like a soothing warm milky drink filling his innards on a winter day.

'That's Micha,' whispered Eva in his ear. 'She's very good at healing things.'

Blanco wanted to reply but he was too busy enjoying the sensation. His arm stopped throbbing so intensely and became instead nothing more than a dull ache.

When he felt the warmth leave him he opened his eyes but didn't feel quite ready to sit up.

'There they are!'

Juan and Rosa da Luega had been first up in the village that morning. It was not yet light but one of their best cows was calving and they wanted to check on her before going to do their normal daily duties. On stepping out of their front door—which faced straight on to the mysterious Count's castle—they were greeted by a most spectacular sight. At first Juan had thought that he was still dreaming but, having asked his wife to pinch him on his arm, the bruise that she left soon proved that he wasn't. The castle was on fire. That would have been enough to delight any villager's eye, for the Count was unwelcome in the area but, even better, the fire was in a variety of colours and was a pleasure to watch for its own sake. Lilac flames shot from the tower, followed by lime green, lemon yellow, and, most spectacular of all, a rainfall of bright shining silver stars.

By this time Juan and Rosa had been joined by the rest of the villagers who were all gaping open-mouthed in astonishment. Sparks and flames from the tower had fallen on to the roof of the castle and it was now ablaze, though with normal orange flames, bright against the darkness of the sky for the village faced into the west—the darkest part of the sky. Then, as the fire took hold of the roof, there was an almighty explosion and the whole castle seemed to disintegrate before their eyes.

'Look!' cried Michel de Angelosa. 'Coming from the tower—there is something there!'

The villagers cried out as one at the sight. Something like a large ungainly bird was flapping its wings away from the blazing tower. It hovered for an instant and then began to plummet to the earth. Something was controlling it though for it did not fall straight down but instead glided like a bird soaring on the wind currents.

Later six-year-old Maria Magdalena da Somorra swore that she saw angels but the adults in the village thought that she had just been over excited by the multi-coloured fire display and thought no more of it.

They had watched where the giant bird fell and, en masse, they ran to find it.

'There they are!'

Blanco and Eva turned to find a whole village-worth of people staring at them as though they had just dropped from heaven.

'Do you think they'll come after us?' asked Eva. 'If they survived, I mean. Griffin said that if his master knew that we had the plans for the fire-powder then he would kill us instantly. His master must have been the Stranger.'

'But the Stranger doesn't know we have the plans,' said Blanco smugly. 'He may well have thought that they went up in flames along with them. At least I hope so.'

'I do hope that Griffin wasn't hurt,' said Eva. Blanco looked at her and she made haste to explain. 'He wanted to help us. It wasn't his fault that you knocked over that astrolabe and brought the Count and the Stranger out.'

'I can't believe,' said Blanco, ignoring her comment about the astrolabe, 'that, after all that, we still don't know who that man is.'

Eva stood up to go to her bed in the house next door with Juan and Rosa. The villagers were a conservative lot and didn't think it right that a boy and girl who were not related should be sleeping under the same roof, even if they had done so for the past few weeks.

'What next I wonder,' she said, stretching.

Blanco didn't look up and his voice was quiet but Eva still heard him clearly enough.

'Barcelona,' was what he said.

Chapter 13

'My feet are sore,' whined Eva.

Blanco sighed. He knew that the problem wasn't that her feet were sore. The problem was that once they crested the next hill Barcelona would be in sight. Eva had walked for weeks to reach the Count's castle without once complaining, but ever since they had left the village she had moaned almost non-stop. And he had to listen to her all on his own for Micha and Azaz had never reappeared after the castle had been destroyed.

The villagers hadn't wanted them to leave. They had been delighted at the destruction of the castle for it had corrupted their view for far too long. The Count himself had not bothered them too much but he had all sorts of strange visitors. And, of course, he had blown up their church.

'But how?' asked Blanco. 'How can a church just blow up?'

Juan shrugged. 'One day it was there as big and solid looking as ever. Then, one night, there was a loud explosion. There were those,' and here he cast a scornful look at Michel, 'who thought the Last Judgement had come. I myself thought that the earth was shaking, like it has done in the past. But when we came out into the street the church was in flames and completely destroyed.'

'But how do you know that it was the Count?' asked Eva, who was with them.

'That man of his, that one who was always covered in rags,' said Juan. 'He had been creeping around that day. Everyone knows it was him.'

'The Count said it was a quarry,' said Blanco.

Juan made a motion of disgust and repeated, 'Everyone knows it was him.'

'Poor Griffin,' said Eva, 'I wonder if he survived the fire.'

They had gone up to the castle later in the day to see if anything or anyone had survived. There was no sign of anyone—not even anything that had ever looked remotely human. Not the Count, the Stranger, Griffin, or even Godoffel.

The castle itself was a wreck. Because the fire had initially started in the tower, when the flames had fallen on to the roof of the castle below they had taken a good hold and the whole roof was gone. Everywhere they looked there were blackened timbers and scorched walls. The tower itself was completely destroyed—not even the staircase remained. On the ground where it had fallen, Eva and Blanco roamed around the rubble, looking for anything that could be useful.

'Ugh! What's this?' Eva held up a jar which had miraculously remained unbroken and which contained something black, wrinkled, and quite freakish looking.

'I don't know,' Blanco replied, looking over her shoulder, 'but I wouldn't bother opening it if I were you.' He looked around him. 'All those plans, all those experiments, that water clock, the beautiful astrolabe—I can't believe they've all gone.'

'Blanco!' cried Eva. 'Look at this!'

Blanco turned to see a small open trunk which was piled full of coins.

'What shall we do with it?' asked Eva in a voice which meant that she would quite like to keep it.

'We have to give it to the villagers,' said Blanco. 'It can help them in rebuilding their church.'

'Oh,' said Eva, trying to mask the disappointment in her voice. 'Of course. What a good idea.'

Blanco continued poking through the rubble. 'I don't know why I'm still looking for Gump's letters. I think I hoped the table might have survived and they might have been in that secret drawer. But maybe the Count had them somewhere else all along.'

'Blanco,' called Eva, sounding slightly strange. 'What do these say?'

She was crouching among the blackened timbers and slowly withdrawing some long strips of parchment. One of the things that Blanco had learnt about Eva on their travels was that she hated that she could not read. Her father had not let her learn and she didn't like it that people could talk about her and pass secrets under her nose and she would be none the wiser.

Blanco took the sheets from her. They were of the same black parchment that his letter from the Count had arrived on with the same neat silvery handwriting on them. They were in scraps with sentences torn off halfway along.

'I think they may be a diary,' said Blanco as he slowly read them. 'Listen. *The boy is getting nearer. Still got the girl with him but . . .* '

'But what?' demanded Eva.

'Don't know,' said Blanco, turning to the next strip.

'It just stopped. I wonder how he knew we were on our way though. This one's about lapis lazuli for some reason. Doesn't make any sense to me. Oh, here's one about the man, the Stranger.'

'He was horrible,' said Eva shivering, 'and he seemed so nice at the beginning. Does it say what his name is?'

'A bit,' said Blanco, 'but it's been smudged by the fire. It's *Luca Ferr* and then I can't read the rest but the Count is wondering why he's suddenly showing so much interest in the flying machines when he didn't care much before.'

'Is that everything?' asked Eva with disappointment in her voice. She had hoped for spells and evidence of sorcery at the very least.

'Just one more,' said Blanco. 'It says, *Rameel is getting stronger*, and then it stops.'

'That's the dark angel,' said Eva. 'But Azaz and Micha have gone off to deal with him. I don't think he'll be back. Azaz is the strongest of them all, you know.'

Blanco said nothing but just gazed at the strips in his hand.

'Do you think they survived?' asked Eva when the silence grew too long.

'I don't know,' replied Blanco slowly. 'They would have had to get down those stairs before the fire took hold.'

'What were those things you threw in the fire?'

'Firecrackers,' answered Blanco with a grin. 'Gump had brought some back from China so I know what they looked like. I don't know how the Count got hold of some.' He paused and then added, 'I hope they didn't get out.'

'But they did get out, didn't they?' asked Micha.

'I think so,' said Azaz. He nodded his head sadly. 'I'm fairly certain they did.'

Azaz and Micha looked at the smoking castle ruins.

'Will they come after Blanco and Eva?' asked Micha.

Azaz shook his head. 'They still don't know that Blanco has the plans for the fire-powder. Blast Rameel,' he added, 'why did he have to encourage them to experiment with that?'

'It was always going to happen,' said Micha. 'Rameel just hurried it along—and gave it to the wrong person.'

'No,' said Azaz, 'they won't come after Blanco. But,' and he looked over to where Blanco and Eva were still searching, 'Blanco may well go after them.'

Micha looked at Azaz. He looked tired and drawn. He had fought a hard battle with Rameel. She reached out and laid her hand on his shoulder.

'Come,' she said. 'It's time to rest.'

They stood on the hill and looked down upon the city of Barcelona. Blanco was excited. It seemed such a long time since he had left Venice and he was looking forward to being in a city again. Also, he had flown—he still couldn't quite believe that he had done that and every time that he remembered he broke out smiling again.

Eva, on the other hand, was looking mutinous. It just wasn't fair, she decided. Blanco had managed to achieve his dream, and he could carry on travelling, or he could go home and run a business, and what did she have to do? Get married to an old man. That was it. That was to be her whole life. She and Blanco had had numerous arguments over it since they had left the castle. He could see no other option. He had to take her to her fiancé's. What, after all, was the alternative? She couldn't keep travelling with him and he couldn't just leave her in the Spanish village as she had begged him to do. So now here they were. Eva heaved a deep sigh and began to follow Blanco down the hill and into the city.

It had been so long since they had been in a city that they had forgotten just how crowded and dirty they could be. Within minutes of passing through the gates they were accosted by beggars demanding alms or food or money. Most were filthy, many of them had limbs covered in dirty bandages. Blanco knew that most of these would prove to be fake could he be bothered to find out, the dried blood often being nothing more than the rust from an old nail. There was dirt and rubbish everywhere and the noise was deafening.

But they had also forgotten the joys of a city. The fact that they could get their hair cut without using Blanco's rough knife, that they could have whatever kind of food they wanted, and that Blanco could send a letter home. He thought that Eva should too—her parents were sure to be extremely worried—but she refused.

They found the Fuggi bank, which had a branch in Barcelona, and Blanco went in to ask them to send a letter home with their next courier.

'Blanco Polo, did you say?' queried the clerk. 'I think I have a letter here for you.'

'Really?' Blanco exclaimed. He didn't think that anyone had known that he was in Barcelona. But it all made sense when he recognized Gump's handwriting. Barcelona had, of course, been where the ship had initially been bound when he had boarded it all those weeks ago.

'What is it?' said Eva when he returned outside to where she was standing.

'Gump has sent me a letter,' he said, tearing it open. It was dated a week after Blanco had left Venice.

'*My dearest Blanco,*' it read. '*What a kerfuffle! You would think no boy had ever left home to go travelling before to judge by your father's reaction. I thought his head was going to explode at one point.*'

Blanco grinned. 'I wish I had been there to see that,' he said and returned to his letter.

'*Your sister, needless to say, was delighted, and has managed to persuade your father that you will be killed and he may as well start teaching her the business. He resisted for a while but has given in. Your mother was distraught but I managed to whisper a word in her ear that you were fine.*

Now, on to the more serious business. I have been hearing some bad things about what Count Maleficio is up to and am thinking that maybe you shouldn't go and help him after all. Apparently he kept some nefarious company while in Venice—sorcerers, alchemists, and the like. Maybe you should just have a little jaunt around Spain and then come home. My letters aren't that important, after all.'

'Well, that's a bit late!' said Eva. 'We've already been!'

'He did think I would be coming to Barcelona

first,' explained Blanco. 'He wasn't to know that I'd get shipwrecked and have to walk the rest of the way.'

'You could have got on another ship, you know,' said Eva. '*I* wasn't stopping you.'

'Yes you were,' Blanco contradicted her. 'You refused to ever set foot on another one and since I was in charge of you, I couldn't leave you.'

'And it was nothing to do with your seasickness?' she asked, her eyes dancing with mischief.

'I feel even worse now that I couldn't find his letters,' he said, quickly changing the topic.

'He says they don't matter,' said Eva.

'I think he's saying that because he thought the Count was dangerous. But I know they meant a lot to him.' He was remembering Gump's face as he had told Blanco about Magdalena. He returned to the letter.

'*I miss you, lad. Nobody else will listen to my stories. Come home. Your loving uncle, Marco.*'

Blanco swallowed a lump that had suddenly appeared in his throat. He had thought of travelling to the southern part of Spain or to the Holy Land where there were lots of inventors but maybe he would go home, after all.

Eva laid a hand on his arm. 'Blanco,' she said, 'would you mind terribly if we didn't go and find my fiancé straight away. Could I just have one night in Barcelona before meeting him?'

Although he would never admit out loud that he might miss her, Blanco found that he didn't like the idea of saying goodbye to Eva, and he hastily agreed.

They had a little difficulty in finding suitable accommodation and when they finally did find a suitable boarding house the landlord explained why they had found it so hard.

'*Fiesta*,' he said abruptly, realizing that they understood little of his language, and therefore wasting as few words as possible on them. '*En el centro*.' And he waved in the general direction of the centre of the city. Looking at each other in delight, they both raced in the direction in which he was pointing.

Smells assaulted them as they wandered through the narrow streets. They were constantly jostled by huge numbers of people all heading in the same direction. Roasting meats, frying vegetables, sweetened fruit all mingled into one delicious combination. On arrival at the square they found the cause of all the delightful smells for the square was surrounded by a host of stalls, all selling their wares and one in every two of them was selling food.

Their mouths were watering and they rushed from stall to stall, smelling everything. They found roasted lamb, beef pies, pork loins, and dumpling. They each had to sample a dish from about five stalls before they could turn their attention to anything in particular. Greedily, Blanco filled his mouth with honeyed wafers when he finally found that stall. Although the villagers had pressed lots of food on them upon their leaving it had, by necessity, been food which would last throughout their travelling and so it had mostly been dried and had little flavour.

'Blanco, look!' cried Eva, her mouth full of dumpling, pointing to the middle of the square where most of the crowd was gathered. 'It's a play!'

They pushed themselves to the front of the crowd and stood looking up at the stage in amazement. It was stories from the Bible that were being played out before the crowd and they had arrived almost at the beginning, at the story of John the Baptist. As Salome began her dance the crowd booed and hissed and Blanco and Eva happily joined in. When she asked for the head of John the Baptist Eva booed loudly and then jumped back in horror as a head was brought with blood running down from the salver on which it was placed.

'Blanco,' she whispered in horror, 'it's not a real head, is it?'

Blanco laughed and shook his head for he had seen many such plays before. Though the effects were always gruesome he knew how many of them were done for he had once befriended one of the players who had shared some of their secrets with him.

But Blanco did not spoil Eva's enjoyment by telling her about them. Instead he watched her clap in delight as Jesus was lifted from his tomb up to the clouds and giggle as Noah's flood inadvertently soaked the front row of spectators. He thought that he had never seen her so happy.

The houses in Señor Massana's part of the city were enormous and beautifully constructed. They were blocked from gazing eyes by having the main part of the house built around an inner courtyard. Señor Massana, whatever faults he may have, was certainly rich and kept a good house. There were vines clambering around the red door on which they knocked. It was answered by a broad-beamed woman who broke into excited broken Italian at sight of them.

Neither Blanco nor Eva could make out anything except that she seemed excited to see them and swept them both inside. Within moments they found themselves seated in a shaded garden with the scent from orange trees filling their nostrils as the woman disappeared back into the house calling on someone.

'Do you think she has mistaken us for someone else?' Blanco asked a little doubtfully.

'I don't think so,' replied Eva. 'I'm sure I heard her mention my name.'

It was mentioned again a moment later and they turned to see a tall, dark young man with deep brown eyes and curling black hair standing in the doorway to the house. Although men were not usually described as such, he was truly beautiful.

'It is Eva di Montini, isn't it?' he asked in flawless Italian. 'My fiancée?'

All Eva could do was nod, her mouth hanging open in surprise. In her mind she had conjured up Señor Massana as much older and uglier. Her fear had been that he would be fat and hairy and would maybe smell. But nothing could have prepared her for this elegant young man who was standing in front of her now.

Blanco felt a strange sick fear in the pit of his stomach as he looked from Señor Massana to Eva and saw them gazing into each other's eyes. He wanted to snatch Eva away and take her back to Venice with him.

Señor Massana walked over to Eva, took her hand, and led her to one of the ornately wrought benches in the garden.

'I have been so worried,' he said, his tone one of deep concern. 'We heard that your ship had been attacked by pirates and feared that you were dead. But then a note arrived, delivered in the middle of the night, saying that you were safe and that you would arrive eventually.'

Blanco tried to catch Eva's eye at this but she was too busy still staring into Señor Massana's eyes. Who could possibly have sent that note? And who was this man? Eva had always said that Señor Massana was old and fat. Had her family misled her?

Señor Massana looked over at Blanco at that point. 'And you must be the Señor Polo who assisted my lovely Eva to arrive here. I am so grateful, señor. You must allow me to pay you for the inconvenience.'

'Eva wasn't an inconvenience,' Blanco said abruptly. 'Anyway, I thought she was to marry someone much older.' He was being rude, he knew, but he didn't like the way Eva was looking at Señor Massana.

Eva glanced over at Blanco at that comment and smiled. Her eyes were shining and her cheeks were flushed. Blanco felt that she was already looking straight through him as though he wasn't really there.

'She was supposed to marry my father,' Señor Massana replied shortly. 'But he died soon after she left Venice. Both families agreed that the match should go ahead and that I should take my father's place.' He glanced at Eva and she smiled at him in delight. 'And now that I have seen how beautiful Eva is, it is now more of a joy than a duty.' Eva beamed at that and Señor Massana smiled in return and then looked at Blanco. 'We must at least give you dinner tonight,' he said. 'I refuse to take no for an answer.'

Blanco fought with himself. He wanted to say no. He wanted to get as far away as possible. But Eva was looking at him pleadingly. She may have fallen in love with Señor Massana at first sight but she was still a stranger in a new house and with a new family to meet. Her eyes begged him to say yes.

'I'll return this evening,' Blanco muttered ungraciously, getting to his feet.

'Of course,' said Señor Massana. 'That will give Eva and me a chance to get to know each other and for her to meet the rest of my family.'

'Could I see Blanco to the door?' she asked Señor Massana. He nodded, as though amused at the request.

'I'll wait for you here, *bonita*,' he said. 'Don't be long.'

Eva blushed at the endearment and then grasped Blanco by the arm and tugged him towards the doorway.

'Blanco,' she whispered. 'Will you do me a favour?'

'Of course,' he said, looking at her with new eyes. Maybe Señor Massana was right. Maybe she was beautiful. She certainly looked it at the moment with her eyes all sparkling like that.

'Don't tell Señor Massana about Azaz and Micha,' she said. 'I couldn't bear it if he thought I was strange and decided not to marry me.'

Blanco laughed in surprise and disappointment. 'I don't think you can cast off angels that easily,' he said. 'Not ones like Azaz and Micha anyway. But I, of course, won't say a word.' Stiffly, formally, he kissed her hand and left.

Dinner was a sumptuous affair. Although Blanco had taken great care to wash and to try to straighten out his best clothes he still didn't look very smart. Eva had been given a whole new set of clothes of blue velvet with silver trim; her hair had been put up and decorated with what Blanco was sure were real jewels. Her eyes were still shining and she barely so much as glanced in his direction. The previous weeks seemed to have been forgotten as she giggled and simpered at her fiancé's side. Blanco knew that he should be happy for her. She had been dreading this so much and, since it was a fate that she could not escape, it was good fortune that it had turned out so much better than she had feared. But Blanco did not feel happy.

There were five of them at dinner—Señor Massana and Eva, Señora Massana, his grandmother, and another woman who was introduced to him as Maria, Señor Massana's cousin. 'Like the Virgin Mother,' she purred. She was gorgeously attired in red silks and wore even more jewels than Eva. Blanco could barely keep his eyes from her at dinner. She made even the simple act of putting food into her mouth into a sensual act. Blanco could not help but notice that Señor Massana could not keep his eyes from her either, although he took great care to talk to Eva throughout the dinner. Blanco also noticed that Maria kept casting glances at Eva—and none of them were friendly.

'Could you pass me some of the honeyed almonds, please?' Eva asked Maria, who was the nearest to them.

Maria gave a deep throaty chuckle and made no move to pass the almonds. Instead she leaned over the table and whispered very loudly to Eva, 'Do you really think you should, my dear. You want to be able to get into your wedding dress, after all.'

Eva looked down at her trencher—which she had

cleared—and then back up at Maria who was gazing at her with a concerned look.

'Perhaps you're right,' conceded Eva.

Señor Massana had overheard and threw Maria an irritated look and placed a comforting hand over Eva's.

'She can eat whatever she wants, Maria,' he snapped. Then he turned and smiled at Eva. 'Nothing could ruin your beauty, *querida*.'

An uncomfortable silence fell. Blanco didn't feel that he should interfere. After a moment the conversation fell back to simple topics—the weather, the neighbours, and what may come of the Count of Barcelona's latest political manoeuvring. They expressed no interest in hearing of Blanco and Eva's journeying. It seemed that they would prefer to forget the unusual way that Eva had arrived at their door. Any time Blanco made an attempt to mention anything relating to their journey the conversation was politely, but very firmly, turned in other directions and so he ended up saying nothing and just ate. But he could taste nothing.

Eva saw him to the door.

'Thank you,' she said simply. 'Thank you for bringing me to Señor Massana's door.' She leaned forward as though to share an intimacy. 'He's so handsome, isn't he?'

Blanco turned from her in disgust and disappointment that the brave, adventuresome girl who had travelled across half the world with him could have turned into this demure, simpering girl just because of one flash of dark eyes and a toss of dark curls. Suddenly Blanco couldn't wait to get away.

Chapter 14

He was wandering aimlessly through the streets the next day, trying not to think of Eva, when a slightly familiar voice hailed him.

'It is Blanco, isn't it?'

He had never seen the couple standing in front of him before in his life. He was sure of it. But she was equally determined that she knew him.

'You don't recognize us, do you?' she said.

Blanco looked at the two of them again. The man was dark of hair; his beard and the hair on his head looked as if they wished to be unruly but did not dare and were trimmed to within an inch of their lives. He was stocky and barrel-chested and had a scar running down his left cheek. She was very tall and thin and her hair was drawn tightly back off her face. She was smiling as she spoke to him and her bright blue eyes sparkled with an enjoyment of life that Blanco didn't share at the moment. Neither of them was young.

'I'm sorry, signora,' Blanco said eventually, having looked his fill, 'but I fear I do not know you, although your voice does sound familiar.'

'Where is my niece?' she asked, smiling. 'Did you deliver her to her fiancé safely?'

'Aunt Hildegard! I didn't recognize you smiling!' Blanco exclaimed in shock and then blushed with embarrassment at his rudeness. Aunt Hildegard only laughed. Now that he looked at her again he could see that it was indeed her. She certainly looked a lot happier than the last time he had seen her. He was amazed that he had ever forgotten her piercing blue eyes. He still had dreams about them forcing him to promise to look after Eva.

'Don't you remember Antonio?' she asked nudging her companion.

Blanco took another look at him and almost fell over. 'You're the pirate captain!' he eventually breathed out.

He nodded and gave Blanco a quick smile, giving a brief glimpse of his gold-capped teeth.

'He's a bit shy,' explained Aunt Hildegard.

'But what . . . ' Blanco spluttered, 'what happened?'

'We fell in love,' she replied simply, gazing into the captain's eyes. Looking somewhat like a lovelorn suitor himself, Antonio, that roguish violent man, gazed back into hers. 'He took me captive and then, over time, it just happened.' She looked at Blanco. 'I'm sure you know what I mean.'

Thinking of Eva Blanco could only nod as he had a large lump in his throat.

'Is Eva with Señor Massana?' she asked him gently.

'She is,' he said, promptly. 'I promised you that I would deliver her and a Polo never breaks his word.'

'I wish I had caught you before you did,' she said. 'When we docked here about a month ago I went to his house and left a letter saying that Eva was safe and would probably turn up here in due time. I thought it was for the best. But now,' she shook her head sorrowfully, 'now I'm not so sure. I have heard bad things about Señor Massana.'

'Like what?' Blanco asked, eager to hear lots of bad things about Señor Massana that he could relate to Eva. He could not forget how she had looked at Señor Massana that first night in the garden. In all the time they had been together, she had never looked at him like that.

Aunt Hildegard leaned towards him so that she could whisper in his ear. 'They say he has a mistress,' she said. 'Her name is Maria. He has only agreed to marry Eva because her father will give him a large dowry and his business is in trouble.'

'Maria!' cried Blanco. 'But we met her. She was at dinner when we dined there. And you say she is his mistress?'

Aunt Hildegard nodded. Blanco was outraged on Eva's behalf. How dare he invite his mistress to his first dinner with his fiancée? How rude!

'We cannot let her marry him,' Blanco said. 'We must stop it!'

Aunt Hildegard laid a hand on his arm. 'I don't think we can, Blanco. Mistresses are, unfortunately, a part of married life. It's not as though couples marry for love. Apart from Antonio and myself, of course. Marriage is primarily a business arrangement, after all.' She squeezed her pirate captain's hand. 'And we cannot help anyway. We sail with the evening tide. We must go.'

'What?' Blanco could not believe that she could tell him all this and then leave. Eva was her niece. Did she not care? And then he realized she was right. Eva may have thought that she was in love with Señor Massana but they were not being married for love. They were being married because Eva's father and Señor Massana's family had arranged it.

'Goodbye, Blanco,' said Aunt Hildegard, shaking his hand. 'Thank you for looking after my niece.' And without a backward glance they were gone.

Eva was feeling a little lonely. She was so used to being with Blanco every moment of the day that it felt strange to be without him. She couldn't even call on the angels for help. Ever since the destruction of the castle they had disappeared. Azaz had said that he needed time to recover from his wounds and Micha had left with him. Eva wondered where angels went to rest. Did they go up to heaven? There were so many things that she had never asked them. What if they never came back?

She stood at the window and looked into the courtyard. She played with the material of her skirt, pleating it between her fingers and then releasing it. She was happy, of course, how could she not be with Señor Massana as her soon-to-be husband? What did it matter if Blanco had never bothered to come and visit her since that first night at dinner? What did it matter if the angels had left her? And what did it matter that she really didn't like any of Señor Massana's family, especially his cousin Maria? With him by her side she was happy.

'Yes, I am,' she said aloud. 'I'm very happy.'

'I'm glad to hear it, *preciosa*,' said the mellifluous tones of Señor Massana from behind her. Unseen by her he had slipped into the room.

She turned in surprise and delight from the window and blushed as she understood his endearment. She would never get used to being told that she was beautiful.

'How are you today, *cariño*?' he asked, crossing the room and placing a quick kiss on her brow.

'I'm a little bored,' replied Eva hesitantly. Was it rude to admit that after all the kindness she had been shown? 'I wondered if I could go out for a walk?'

'By yourself?' cried Señor Massana in horror. 'No respectable young lady ever goes out for a walk by herself.'

Eva had a sudden recollection of her Aunt Hildegard and wondered what had happened to her. She hoped that her suffering hadn't lasted long after the pirates had boarded the ship.

'Maybe my cousin, Maria, will accompany you later,' added Señor Massana when he saw Eva's disappointment.

Eva hesitated but she was too unused to keeping her feelings hidden to start now.

'I don't think I like your cousin,' she said defiantly. 'She treats me like a child.'

Señor Massana threw back his head and laughed, showing all his teeth. 'Then you needn't walk with her,' he said.

'But what shall I do all day?' asked Eva plaintively.

'Talk to me,' said Señor Massana with a smile that dissolved all of Eva's worries and left her content.

Blanco wandered disconsolately through the streets of Barcelona thinking of Eva. What to do now? Did he really want to go home? He wished he had the angels to talk things over with but then he could never really talk to them except when Eva was near.

He looked up as something caught his eye.

Something that looked incredibly like a long flowing silvery cloak. It disappeared around the corner before Blanco could get a proper look but he was sure that he had seen it. And there was only one person he knew who wore a cloak like that.

He ran to the corner but when he looked round he saw lots of people but none of them were wearing a long silver cloak. Had he been imagining it? Had he been thinking so much about his travels that he only thought he saw the Count? But then, they had never found any proof that he had died.

Wandering further, he found himself down at the docks. Here he felt incredibly homesick. It reminded him too much of Venice. He missed his mother and Gump. He missed his friends. He missed Venice itself. He longed to hear the sound of the Arsenal again.

He asked around and finally found the captain of a ship sailing for Venice. The villagers had insisted that he and Eva had to take a share of the gold they had found as a reward for getting rid of the Count for them. Therefore Blanco could afford not to work his passage home this time, for which he was truly grateful. He was negotiating for a cabin with the captain when he caught sight of a sumptuous ship, larger than all the rest, and heavily laden with cargo. But it wasn't that that had attracted his attention.

'Where's that one bound?' Blanco asked.

The captain gave it a glance. 'Acre,' he said. 'Lovely ship, isn't she? No one knows who she belongs to. You looking for a berth?'

'Yes, to Venice,' said Blanco, not taking his eyes from the larger ship.

'I've got just the one cabin left,' said the captain. He named his price.

'Fine,' said Blanco, handing it over without an argument. The captain was astonished. He had expected him to haggle but he wasn't going to argue, not when he had the money in his hand. 'I'll make sure it's all spruced up for you.' He didn't know who this passenger was but if he was this happy to hand out money so easily then the captain was more than happy to welcome him aboard.

'When do you sail?' asked Blanco.

'With the evening tide on the morrow,' replied the captain. 'If we miss that one then we can't leave for a couple of days. Are you travelling alone?' he asked.

Blanco paused and then nodded. 'Yes,' he said. 'I'm travelling alone. I'll join your ship just before she sails.'

The captain nodded happily and reiterated that they had to sail with the evening tide. Blanco nodded and glanced again at the bigger ship before turning and walking away from the docks back into the main centre of Barcelona. He had made up his mind. But first he was going to find Eva and say goodbye.

He stopped off first to break his fast for his day had started early and he had yet to eat. Leaning against a stall in the main square of Barcelona, Blanco nearly dropped his food. At a stall across the square was the Stranger and he was talking to a woman who looked very like Señor Massana's mistress, Maria. Taking care not to be seen, Blanco made his way across the square and settled himself behind a pillar close by. He sneaked a quick look at them.

The Stranger looked almost exactly the same as when Blanco had last seen him in the tower room. He was smiling in that particular way that he had and nodding his head as Maria whispered urgently in his ear. She was dressed in dark red velvet—the colour of blood, Blanco couldn't help thinking. He felt incredibly uncomfortable even looking at her after what Aunt Hildegard had told him. If he strained, he could just make out what they were saying. He listened open-mouthed with his hand clapped over his mouth in case he called out in disgust at what he was hearing.

Eventually the Stranger rose from his chair. 'That is my final offer,' he said.

'Then I think we have a deal,' said Maria, rising in one fluid movement from her own seat.

'When can I get the girl?' asked the Stranger.

'After the wedding,' said Maria and then she laughed. 'With my blessing.'

Blanco leaned against his pillar. 'Azaz!' he called, looking upwards. 'If you can hear me, I really need you now.'

Blanco knocked on the door to Señor Massana's house. It remained steadfastly shut. He hammered again and this time, after a moment, he heard quick footsteps and a manservant opened the door. He looked at Blanco with disgust and Blanco made haste to ease his breathing and stand up straight. It made no difference to the man's expression. He said nothing.

'I wish to see Señorita Eva di Montini,' said Blanco.

The man continued to stare, saying nothing.

'Señor Massana's fiancée?' said Blanco.

There was a sharp command from behind the man and he stepped aside. Blanco found himself looking at Señora Massana.

'Eva is resting,' she said, smiling at him sweetly. 'She won't be able to see anyone. She is in seclusion until her wedding.'

'She'll see me,' said Blanco confidently. 'I want to say goodbye to her.'

'You're leaving Barcelona?' she asked, raising her eyebrows in surprise. She eyed him coolly and then she nodded as if she had made a decision.

'Won't you come in?' she asked, opening the door wider. 'I can offer you some refreshments. But I can't promise that you will be able to see Eva.'

Blanco shook his head vigorously. He knew that he didn't want to enter that house.

'When is the wedding to take place?' he asked.

'Tomorrow,' replied Señora Massana. 'I am sorry that we cannot invite you but it is a purely family affair, you understand. Our family chapel is not large. It cannot hold many people.'

Blanco nodded and backed down the steps, almost falling over in his haste to get away. 'Tell Eva I said goodbye!' he called and ran down the street.

'Wait!' called Señora Massana after him. 'Where shall I tell her you're going?'

She received no reply.

Chapter 15

Eva was distinctly cross. After the freedom of her travels she had found the restrictions of living in a proper house and having to be chaperoned wherever she went to be extremely constricting. Also she was annoyed that Blanco seemed to have made no attempt whatsoever to see her. They had travelled together for weeks and it would appear that he had left her without a backward glance, without even a message. Since that meal on their second night in Barcelona she hadn't seen or heard anything from him. She didn't know if he was even still in Barcelona.

She sighed loudly. She didn't like Señor Massana's grandmother—she was always cross and demanding and his cousin, Maria, seemed always to be in the house. Eva definitely didn't like her. She thought her laugh was condescending and she kept stroking Señor Massana's arm. If Señor Massana hadn't been so handsome and kind to her, Eva didn't know what she would have done. She couldn't wait to marry him. Then she could run the house and that Maria would never get to set foot in it again.

She fidgeted. Her knees hurt and her dress was too tight across her chest. She looked down at it. It was the most beautiful dress she had ever owned— even better than the one that the Count had given her. It was red and covered with gold embroidery.

On the sleeves and across the bodice were hundreds of tiny little pearls. She supposed that it was fitting that her wedding dress should be so beautiful.

She fidgeted again. She wasn't entirely sure why she had asked if she could pray in the private chapel before the ceremony. If it wasn't that Azaz and Micha had never reappeared after the castle, she could have sworn that Micha had whispered the suggestion in her ear. She sighed. She missed the angels, although she couldn't deny that her life was infinitely easier without them.

'Eva!'

The whisper was loud across the heavy silence in the chapel.

Eva whipped her head round but she could see nothing.

'Eva! Over here! Come to the door!'

Eva was certain that she knew that voice. She looked around surreptitiously but there was no one else in the chapel. She had asked to pray privately and it seemed her wish had been granted. She stood up, sighing in relief as the life came back to her knees, and crossed over to the door. It was barred from her side for it opened on to the side streets.

'Who is it?' she hissed.

'By all the saints,' came the impatient voice, 'if you don't know my voice by now . . . '

Eva shoved aside the bolt and pulled open the door slightly. There, as she had suspected, stood Blanco. He was still dressed in his travelling clothes. After spending a week in the Massanas' gloriously attired household, Eva couldn't help noticing how dusty and dirty he looked.

'It's my wedding day,' she said, pulling open the door a little more and showing him her dress. 'Have you come to say goodbye?' Her voice got a little crosser. 'Why haven't you been to see me before? You haven't even sent me any messages.'

'Yes, I have,' said Blanco, looking grim. 'They obviously didn't pass them on. Every time I came to see you they said you were resting.'

'Oh,' she said. 'I'm sure there must have been some misunderstanding. I bet it was that horrible Maria.'

Blanco didn't look convinced.

Eva pouted. 'You haven't said that you like my dress,' she said, twirling round.

Blanco rolled his eyes in disbelief and wondered whether the old Eva that he knew had disappeared completely and whether this one was worth saving.

On the far side of the chapel, approaching footsteps could be heard. Someone was coming in.

'Eva!' hissed Blanco. 'You must stop them coming in. If they see me, they'll . . . ' He trawled for words in his mind that he could say without frightening her but could think of none. 'They might not let me talk to you. Just do it for me, please. Just ask for a few more moments.'

'Eva!' It was the cross voice of Señora Massana that could be heard. 'Are you ready?' She rattled the door. Blanco gave Eva a push in that direction. She gave him an annoyed look but she ran across and caught the door as Señora Massana pushed it open.

'Just a few more moments, Mama Massana,' Blanco could hear her saying to the other woman. 'If you don't mind. I shan't be long.'

'See that you aren't,' snapped the señora. 'We have a lot to do today.'

They could hear her grumbling as she retraced her steps back along the corridor. Eva pulled a face.

'She's horrible,' she said. 'So is his cousin, Maria. Only Señor Massana is nice and I suppose I won't have to bother with the others once I've married him.'

Blanco snorted.

'Are you going to stay for the wedding?' asked Eva.

'No,' said Blanco. 'And neither are you.'

And on that word he grabbed Eva's arm and pulled her out of the chapel.

'Let go of me!' she cried. 'What are you doing?'

Blanco ignored her, shut the door of the chapel, and half carried, half dragged her along the street. She did her best to pull back. The side street was empty and there was no one to hear her cries but as they approached the main road her crying would pose a problem. There were a lot of people about and if they caught sight of a scruffy boy dragging along a well dressed young woman then they would be surrounded immediately.

'Eva, please shut up!' pleaded Blanco. 'You've got to trust me. I promise I'll tell you everything once we get away from here.'

'No!' cried Eva. 'I want to marry Señor Massana. You're just jealous.'

'Of course I'm not,' scoffed Blanco, as if the thought had never entered his head. 'But please do be quiet.'

'No.'

'Eva,' said a voice that she knew well. 'Eva, you must be quiet.'

'Azaz!' she cried. 'Oh Azaz, I've missed you. Is Micha with you?'

'I'm here,' said Micha. 'But trust Blanco, Eva. And please be quiet.'

Eva was quiet. Blanco looked around at the side street behind him. He knew that they would go to the chapel soon to prepare Eva for the wedding. They didn't have long.

'You'll have to walk on ahead,' he said. 'I'll have to pretend to be your servant otherwise people will stare.'

'Very well,' said Eva. 'But you'd better have a really good explanation for this. And you'd better get me back in time for my wedding. Now, where am I heading?'

'To the docks,' said Blanco.

'Well, here we are,' she said, a while later, her calm voice belying her anger. 'You've ruined my wedding day and I'm hiding behind a crate in the middle of the docks. You'd better start talking—and fast!'

She sounded furious. Blanco wasn't quite sure where to begin.

'Maria,' he said hesitantly. 'I saw her talking with the Stranger.'

Eva paled. She hadn't been expecting to hear about him again. But then she looked down at her wedding dress and thought of Señor Massana's deep brown eyes gazing at her adoringly and so instead of being curious she shouted, 'She's a trouble-maker that woman. Maybe it wasn't even really him!'

'Of course it was him!' cried Blanco. 'I'm hardly going to mistake him, am I? Last time I saw him he wanted to kill us! He still does! And Maria was shaking hands with him and talking to him. And I saw the Count. And yesterday when I was here I saw Griffin up on that ship!'

He pointed to the large ship bound for Acre which he had been looking at the day before. It was ready to sail. It was obviously just waiting for one last something or someone. As they looked a man came out of the cabin and stood looking impatiently at the entrance to the docks. Blanco and Eva watched from behind the crate. The man was very tall, very thin, and was wearing a long silver cloak.

'This has nothing to do with me,' said Eva, looking stubbornly away from the ship and refusing to look Blanco in the eye. 'It was you who stole the plans. It was you who wanted to fly that stupid machine. It was you who burnt the castle down. It's you they're after. Not me!'

'Oh, really,' said Blanco angrily. 'Then why did your fiancé arrange to sell you to the Stranger then?'

Eva stared at him in shock and disbelief.

Blanco cursed. He had really hoped that he wasn't going to have to mention that bit. He had thought she might just be scared enough that the Stranger was in Barcelona.

'What do you mean?' asked Eva, her bottom lip quivering, however hard she tried to stop it. 'I thought you said it was Maria who met him, not Señor Massana.'

'I eavesdropped,' he said. 'Maria said that Señor Massana agreed to sell you after he'd married you. That way he'd have both the money from your dowry and the money that the Stranger would pay to take you.'

'But . . . but . . . ' said Eva, one small tear escaping from her eye and trickling down her cheek. 'I thought he really liked me. He acted like he did. Maybe it was just Maria. Maybe he knew nothing about it!'

Blanco weighed up how much to tell her. From what he had heard Señor Massana had always intended to marry Eva for her dowry and then lock her away and ensconce Maria as mistress in his house. But when he found someone who would offer to take Eva away he was even more delighted. His only stipulation had been that the marriage should take place first so that he could legitimately claim Eva's dowry. Blanco felt a small spark of satisfaction that he had been right about Señor Massana all along but as he looked at Eva's disconsolate face he tempered the truth.

'I'm sure he did,' said Blanco. 'But I think he likes Maria even more.'

Eva drew in a sharp breath and then sank down again on the crate.

'That horrible woman,' she said angrily. 'She was always there. She never left me alone with him.' She leaned against the crate. 'They'll come after me when they find I'm not in the chapel,' she said in horror. 'They'll know you took me. What will we do? I don't want to marry him now!'

'I don't know.'

There was a pause and then Eva said, in a confused voice, 'But why did the Stranger want me and not you? Did he think if he took me that you would follow? And of course, he would know where to find me because I made no secret about who I was marrying.' She continued thinking aloud. 'So that all makes sense. But what I don't understand is why he would want either of us?'

Blanco debated with himself whether to tell her or not. He opened his mouth to answer when a sudden loud commotion at the entrance to the docks caused them to look round in surprise. A group of horsemen appeared. It was Señor Massana, the Stranger, and a group of household retainers, and from what they could see through the slats of the crate, Señor Massana was looking furious. The Stranger was beaming as usual but Blanco could tell that he was not happy.

'Quick!' said Blanco, pulling Eva to her feet. 'Get into this crate before they come over here.'

They both clambered into the crate. It wasn't easy. It was half full of wool but there was just enough room for them both. It was hot and scratchy and very smelly but it was better than being on the docks.

They watched the proceedings open mouthed through the open slats. It was almost like watching a play, only in this one Blanco didn't think there would be any fancy tricks when it came to rivers of blood. Señor Massana and the Stranger were arguing furiously while the servants were searching along the docks. Blanco and Eva could hear only snatches of conversation.

'. . . even keep control . . . girl!'

'. . . that boy . . . Blanco.'

'. . . sail with this tide.'

Señor Massana shouted some more orders to his servants and they began to be much more rough in their search, kicking over crates as they went and pulling hoods from people's heads.

'Blanco,' said Eva quietly. 'I'm scared.'

He put an arm around her shoulder and pulled her closer to him. He kept his eyes firmly fixed on what was happening on the docks.

Some of the sailors were getting annoyed at the rough treatment of Señor Massana's servants and they started shouting and pushing some of them. One blow led to another. Soon a full scale fight was taking place. Their own crate was pushed backwards as one of the sailors fell on to it as he fought with one of Señor Massana's men. Eva gasped and Blanco whispered at her to be quiet.

He could still see the Stranger and he breathed a sigh of relief when he eventually turned away from Señor Massana in disgust and stalked up the gangplank to the ship where he was joined on deck by the Count. The gangplank was lifted and Blanco could hear the orders being given to set sail.

Blanco and Eva were clutching hands in relief when they suddenly felt their crate being lifted. Their delight changed to horror as they were swung around.

'This one's heavy,' said a guttural voice. 'Must have a whole sheep in it!'

The other man grunted, obviously finding the load hard to carry.

Through the slats Eva and Blanco watched as they passed along the dock. The fight was still raging between about half the people there while the other half were loading ships as though fights were such a normal part of their daily routine that they didn't even notice one was going on. They would skip out of the way as punches were swung or dodge round a couple grappling on the ground.

Blanco and Eva knew they couldn't risk jumping out for Señor Massana was still there and the Stranger's ship was only just slipping out of its mooring and could be called back easily. Eva held her breath as they were carried right past Señor Massana. If she had stretched out her hands she could have touched him. She bit back a small sob as they passed.

Their crate was carried up the gangplank of a small ship and dumped amongst a pile of other crates. There were lots of sailors around and the cargo area was constantly full of people so they remained stuck for the moment. Thankfully no other crates were put on top of them but they were stacked all around them, caging them in.

'We can sneak out later,' said Blanco in a confident voice. 'They'll have one last drink in town maybe before they set sail.'

'Hurry up!' they heard the man who had carried them aboard say. 'We've got to set off with this tide or who knows when we'll leave.'

The sound of sails being raised and the clinking of irons as the anchor was lifted filtered through to the pair in the crate. It was dark in there and they couldn't see each other's faces but they were still holding hands, drawing a little comfort from each other's presence.

The sounds continued around them and it really seemed that they would have no chance to escape from their self imposed prison.

'Maybe we should just climb out,' said Eva, 'and tell them the problem.'

'No,' said Blanco, holding on tightly to her arm in case she decided to suit her actions to her words. 'Let's just wait a bit. If they see us they may shout out and draw attention to us. I'd rather travel out to sea in a crate than be captured by the Stranger.'

Eva couldn't help but see the sense in this although she had to squash a small hope that maybe if Señor Massana caught sight of her in her wedding dress he might change his mind. To take her mind off this she carried on talking.

'Blanco,' she whispered. 'You were going to tell me about why they want us. I know you were. I could tell by your face.'

She could feel Blanco hesitate and then he said, 'They didn't want *us*, Eva, they wanted you.'

'Oh,' she said, not expecting that. Blanco had been the leader of their trip all the way, had made all the decisions, had been the reason that they had been at the Count's castle all along. She had never meant to be there in the first place, so why would they want her?

'Initially, the Count wanted me,' explained Blanco, having learnt all this from listening to the Stranger and Maria. 'He wanted me to help him finish the flying machine for . . . well, you know what for. But when they found out about your angels, then the Stranger decided that he wanted you.'

'Wait a moment,' said Eva, 'do you still not know his full name?'

'No,' said Blanco with frustration, 'Maria never mentioned it once during their talk.'

'So they want the angels?' Eva asked.

'No,' said Blanco. 'Well, yes, they think the angels will follow you. But he wants you because you can talk to them.'

'So can you,' said Eva, 'well, to Azaz at least.'

'Yes, but I can't see them and you can. The Stranger thinks that you have special powers.'

'Really?' said Eva, torn between pride at having special powers and fright at the thought that they were after her because of them. 'I wonder what—'

'Fully loaded, sir!' came a shout from just outside their crate, causing them both to jump.

'All ready!' shouted the first mate. 'Everyone and everything aboard!'

'Then let's set sail!' called the captain. 'Set course for Venice!'

'Course for Venice!' repeated the steersman.

Blanco and Eva could only look at each other with delight. Venice, despite all the problems it held, meant, for now, home and safety.

Blanco reached out and took Eva's hand. 'I'm sorry I ruined your wedding day,' he said.

Eva shrugged. 'I never really liked him anyway,' she said blatantly lying. 'I was just pretending so that you wouldn't have to feel guilty about leaving me.'

Blanco was about to tell her that that was arrant nonsense because he had seen the way that she had looked at Señor Massana but he saw her bottom lip just begin to tremble and so he squeezed her hand instead.

'At least I have a good excuse to tell my parents why I'm not married,' continued Eva and then she sighed. 'Although they may not believe me and they're sure to think it's all my fault. Especially when I tell them that Aunt Hildegard died in a pirate attack.'

'But, Eva,' said Blanco, raising his voice in his excitement. 'I knew I had something good to tell you. She didn't. Die, I mean. I met her. She was the one who told me to watch out for Maria. She's married to Antonio.'

'Who?'

'The pirate captain.'

'No!' said Eva. 'My aunt Hildegard—with a pirate captain!' She paused and then whispered in a shocked tone, 'Blanco, you don't think he forced her, do you?'

'I don't think so,' said Blanco. 'She looked pretty happy to me. If anything, I would say she forced him.'

'Well, well,' said Eva, smiling. 'Looks like I will no longer be the most disreputable member of my family when I get home.'

'I got to fly,' said Blanco, adding to the tally. 'And my journey was even more exciting than Gump's.'

Blanco thought of Gump's letters. Going home without them meant that he would never hear the full story of his great-uncle and Magdalena but maybe Gump would relent when he heard of Blanco's adventures or maybe if he got Eva to ask him. Her insatiable questions were enough to make even Gump give in.

He touched Eva's arm.

'Eva,' he said. 'How would you like to meet my great-uncle Marco?'

Before he could clap his hand over her mouth, Eva shrieked with delight.

A moment later and they were looking at blue sunshine as a sailor wrenched off the top of the crate.

'What do we have here then?' he said, looking down at them and not appearing too happy at seeing them. He turned away. 'Captain!'

Blanco stood up and stretched out his cramped limbs. At least they were at sea. He looked around him. Far off to his right he could see a large golden ship, its sails fluttering in the stiff breeze that was carrying it further and further away from their own ship. He breathed a sigh of relief.

'Well, well,' came a rough voice from behind him. 'Two little stowaways. I hope you can swim because you're going overboard.'

Blanco turned to find the captain of the ship with whom he had haggled a passage home the previous day.

'It's you!' said the captain in some surprise. 'This is an unusual way to travel. You did pay for a cabin after all.' He caught sight of Eva still crouching in the crate. His eyes narrowed suspiciously. 'You didn't say you were bringing a girl with you though. And especially not one in her wedding dress.'

'Sudden change in plans,' said Blanco smoothly. 'We just got married.'

Eva looked at him in surprise and then shrugged. What did it matter what he said? They were going home.

The Adventure Continues . . .

September 2005

ISBN 0 19 271963 7

'Can you swim?'

'Well, actually, yes,' said Blanco, trying to look modest and failing. He was quite proud of his ability to swim as he knew that not many people could.

'You see that island there?' The captain of the ship pointed off to the left, where a cliff rose from sea level up.

Blanco nodded.

'Could you swim that far?' the captain asked.

Blanco nodded enthusiastically.

'Excellent,' said the captain. He turned to the burly seaman standing behind him. 'Toss him over.'

'What?' spluttered Blanco.

'Toss him over,' repeated the captain, walking away. 'And the girl with him.'

The ship got smaller and smaller until eventually it disappeared altogether.

The water lapping around their feet was warm and a beautiful shade of blue. They were standing on a rocky ledge with only a small climb behind them to take them on to the headland. The sun beat down mercilessly on their heads. The girl looked at the cliff to find a place to start climbing but the boy kept staring out to sea, as though willing the ship to return.

'It's gone,' said Eva.

'I know,' said Blanco, through gritted teeth.

'I'm sorry,' she continued, although, truth be told, she didn't look that sorry.

'Stop saying that,' growled Blanco.

'Well, what else can I say?'

'Nothing!' shouted Blanco. 'And if you hadn't said anything in the first place then we wouldn't be here. We'd be halfway home to Venice.'

As hard as she tried to prevent it, Eva couldn't stop a tiny flicker of triumph from curling her lips up. Blanco may have been in a hurry to get to Venice but she certainly wasn't. She quickly glanced at him but he had missed her smile, which was probably just as well since he was already in a foul mood. She wrung out her wet dress as she stared back at him.

'I didn't mean it,' she said defensively.

'Well, the captain thought you did,' said Blanco, 'and, more to the point, so did his crew.' He glared at her. 'And now we could be anywhere and we're soaking wet.'

'It wasn't completely my fault,' said Eva. 'Azaz told me to say it.'

Micha turned abruptly to the angel sitting beside her.

'Did you make her say it?' she asked.

'Of course,' said Azaz complacently. 'It was as plain as, well, the nose on your face, and I knew it would upset him. And I had to get them off the boat somehow. You know that.'

Micha shook her head. 'Oh, Azaz,' she said, 'that could almost count as interference.'

Azaz grinned, unperturbed by what she said. 'No, no. I didn't make *her say it. I only suggested it.'*

Micha looked at Azaz as he sat on the rocks beside Eva. He was polishing his gold belt as he spoke and his red robes were like a blanket of anemones covering the rocks. He winked at her and patted the rock next to him.

She smiled and sat down.

The ship had disappeared completely now and any hope that Blanco may have had that the captain might change his mind and come back for them had disappeared with the last flutter of its sails. He continued gazing angrily out to sea, partly so that he wouldn't have to talk to Eva. They had finally been on their way home to Venice and now they were further away than ever! At least in Barcelona, where they had boarded the ship, there had been other ships or they could have walked home. It might have taken a long time but it could have been done. But to be stuck on an island was something different altogether. What if they never got off?

'Oh, this is hopeless,' said Blanco eventually, turning away from the sea and looking up at the cliff. 'Well, I suppose there's nothing else for it but to go and try to find someone who can tell us where we are. At least the captain said the island was inhabited.'

Eva bit her lip and debated with herself whether to tell Blanco the last bit of what the captain had said. Blanco had already been tossed overboard by that point and so hadn't heard. He had indeed said that this part of the island was inhabited but then he had added, 'by pirates.' She decided not to. Blanco would only blame her. She watched him as he started to climb.

'Where are we, Azaz?' she whispered.

'Malta,' he said in his normal voice, knowing that Blanco couldn't hear him.

Eva gave a start and almost stumbled back down the slope.

'What are you doing?' asked Blanco impatiently as he glanced down at her. 'Put your feet where mine were. It's not difficult.'

'I just slipped a little,' said Eva, in such a subdued tone that Blanco should have known that she wasn't telling the truth. Subdued was not normally in her nature. However, he was too cross with her to listen to her properly.

'Malta,' she whispered under her breath when Blanco had started scrambling up the cliff again. 'Are you sure?'

'Oh yes,' he said. 'I picked it particularly.'

'I knew it!' said Eva, a little louder. 'I knew you had made me say that to the captain.'

'What?' said Blanco, looking back again.

'I didn't make you,' said Azaz. 'I just pointed it out.'

'Nothing,' said Eva, motioning Blanco upwards. 'I'm just talking to Azaz about something.' She didn't want to tell Blanco where they were. He had mentioned Malta to her before. It was where his great-uncle Marco Polo had visited after his travels. It seemed very strange that it was where they had ended up.

Blanco sighed and continued upwards. He had enough to worry about without wondering what Eva was saying to her angels. He wanted to go home. Instead of having a lovely, exciting adventure, building a flying machine and then going home to tell his great-uncle all about it, he had already been away twice as long as he had expected. Now, they were on the run from the Count and his nasty accomplice, the Stranger, and stuck on a pink island.

'And it *is* pink,' he muttered as he finally stumbled over the top of the cliff and gazed about him. 'Very pink.'

It was also one of the flattest, most barren places he had ever seen. Even whole stretches of the north Spanish countryside through which he had walked had been less barren than this. Everywhere was scrubland and all with a pink tinge and the sun was so hot. Desperately he looked around for a tree under which to shade but there was nothing bigger than a large bush. He turned to look down at Eva. She was still muttering furiously under her breath to the angels. He couldn't always see them. When he had first met her he hadn't believed in them at all and had thought that she was touched by the moon when she said that she had two angels who followed her around. Normally only holy women could talk to angels and no one who had ever met Eva would have thought her a holy woman. But since then he had spoken to Azaz and once he had thought he had even seen him.

He reached down and pulled her over the top.

'Isn't it lovely?' she said, with a brilliant smile. 'What a beautiful island!'

'It's pink,' said Blanco with a frown, 'and it looks uninhabited. The captain promised that he wouldn't leave us on a deserted island but I think this one is.'

'Oh, I don't think so,' said Eva. 'I'm sure we'll find someone. Look, there's a church over there.'

'Where?'

'Up on the hill. You can hardly see it. It seems to be made of the same colour as the earth.'

'Well, at least we might get some shade there.'

By the time they reached the church Blanco thought that he might melt with the heat. The good thing was that it had dried their clothes. Soon they were inside the church and settled into the nearest pew. Blanco was determined that not a drop of sunlight should cross his path. Once there, he sighed.

'Blanco?' said Eva hesitantly. Was this the time to mention the fact that they were on Malta.

'What?' he snapped.

No, not a good time.

'I think there's someone coming,' she said instead.

Blanco could hear the crunch of the stones on the path which led to the church. Whoever it was, was slow and heavy footed.

'We'd better hide,' Eva continued, looking round for the best place in which to do so.

'Why would we want to hide? I thought the whole point of us being here was to find someone so that they could tell us where we are and maybe help us.'

'Well, yes,' said Eva, looking nervous. The footsteps were getting nearer, 'but what you didn't hear the captain saying was that this part of the island was mainly inhabited by pirates.'

'What!' cried Blanco, leaping to his feet. 'Why didn't you tell me?'

He grabbed her arm and dragged her behind the nearest pillar. They were just in time for, as the last flutter of Eva's skirt disappeared, the church door screeched open. They could see only an outline in the doorway as the sun, streaming in behind the person, turned him into a shadow. Slowly he shuffled his way forward, aiming determinedly for the front. His progress was slow and staggered.

'He doesn't look like a pirate!' hissed Eva.

'Sssh! He'll hear you,' said Blanco, as memories of the last set of pirates they had met swept over him. There had been a lot of blood and violence. He really didn't want to meet another one—ever!

The man came level with their pillar and they saw him properly for the first time. He was old and bowed and his hands shook slightly.

'Blanco, he is not a pirate,' hissed Eva, louder than before. The old man made no appearance of having heard her and continued on his way to the front. 'He's just a harmless old man.'

'You said that about the Stranger,' said Blanco. Eva could only sigh in agreement. The Stranger had seemed such a jolly old man, always smiling and chatting away to her as though her opinion had really mattered. But he had turned out to be evil and so Eva was beginning to doubt her judgement about people. But still . . .

'Blanco, he's leaning on a stick and I don't think he can see very well.'

'Well, let's just see what he's up to,' said Blanco, who had definitely learned never to take anyone at face value ever again.

As they watched, the old man shuffled up to a casket which lay across the front of the altar. He bent over it as though in prayer but both Blanco and Eva jumped when he suddenly pushed the lid, which fell to the floor with a thunderous clatter.

'You see,' hissed Blanco. 'He *is* a pirate and that's where he keeps all his treasure.'

Eva rolled her eyes but kept her thoughts to herself.

The old man was now scrabbling about in the contents of the casket. With a small cry of triumph he finally found what he was looking for. With a few more little cries of delight, he lifted his spoils to his lips and started to gnaw on them.

'Eurgh!' said Blanco. 'What *is* he doing?'

Silence greeted his question and, with a sinking feeling, Blanco realized that Eva was no longer beside him which meant she was . . .

'What do you think you are doing?' It was Eva at her most stentorian. The old man jumped and turned to face her, still with his mouth full. Blanco groaned. Now they were in the middle of it. Again.

'Stop laughing, Azaz,' said Micha, trying to stifle a smile of her own.

'I can't,' he said. 'Look at Blanco's face.'

Micha turned to look. Blanco's face was a mix of outrage, frustration, and fear. He was popping in and out from behind the pillar as though he couldn't quite decide whether to join Eva or leave her alone.

'This is all your fault,' said Micha. 'I hope you know what you're doing.'

'I always know what I'm doing,' said Azaz, settling himself in a pew and watching Eva. 'I thought you knew that by now.'

'That is a holy relic,' said Eva, with outrage in every tone. 'Why are you trying to eat it?'

The old man merely stared at her, his jaw still working at the bone of the finger that he was trying to gnaw from the holy relic's hand. He was dirty and unkempt looking. His robes, which looked as though they had once been of the finest materials, were now threadbare and tattered and draped loosely on his scrawny body. The eyes, which had fixed on Eva, even as he continued chewing, were red-tinged and staring.

'Stop it!' she cried. When the man ignored her, she moved forward, not particularly keen on the idea of touching either the holy relic or the old man. Just as she was reaching out to grab the relic, her hand was seized from behind.

'What are you doing?' hissed Blanco. 'You can't touch a holy relic.'

'Well, he is,' said Eva, motioning with her untrapped hand at the man, who had turned away from them. The finger was proving obstinate and he was having trouble gnawing it from the hand to which it was attached.

'That's got nothing to do with us,' retorted Blanco.

'He's doing it right in front of us,' argued Eva. 'We can't just ignore him.'

'Yes, we can,' said Blanco. 'We have enough problems of our own to deal with.'

Eva ignored him and turned back to the man. 'Stop that!' she said to him. 'Put that down at once!'

Surprised by her peremptory tone, the man stopped gnawing for a moment. His teeth remained bared: long, strong, yellow teeth. Then he started chewing again. Eva reached out and grabbed his arm. He ignored her.

'You see,' said Blanco. 'Just leave him be.'

'But . . .'

What Eva was about to say remained unsaid as

the church door screeched open one more time and a tall woman in a nun's habit came striding up the aisle.

'Put that down at once,' she said in such a strict tone that Blanco dropped his pack and Eva dropped the old man's arm as though it had scalded her. The old man, on the other hand, carried on as before.

A glimmer of a smile crossed the nun's lips at the sight of the two stunned faces gazing at her. Then she quickly corrected her expression and frowned. She strode past Eva and Blanco, picked up the casket lid and slid it back on. Just before his fingers were trapped between the lid and the hard sides, the old man let go of the bone he was holding and shuffled back. She grabbed hold of his arm and started dragging him down the aisle. When she was halfway down she turned.

'Well,' she said, 'are you coming or aren't you?'

'Malta!'

The abbess looked surprised at the vehemence of Blanco's response to her reply to his question.

Blanco looked around the room as though searching for a map to prove that she was correct. His gaze finally landed on Eva, who was trying her best to look as surprised as he was. It wasn't working. He narrowed his eyes at her but decided he would question her later. He turned back to the abbess, who was looking at him with a raised eyebrow.

'Can I ask where you were bound?' she asked.

'Venice,' said Blanco.

'But we're not in a hurry to get there,' said Eva. 'I would quite like to stay for a while, if that would be possible. Only, we don't have any money and . . . '

'That would be perfectly possible,' interrupted the abbess smoothly. 'You are welcome to stay for as long as you like. You will not be surprised to hear that we don't get many visitors here. One thing I don't understand, though, is how you got here.'

'We were thrown off a ship,' said Eva, 'by a very rude man.'

'I don't think he was the only one being rude,' said Blanco. 'What you said was very rude.'

'What did you say?' asked the abbess. Her face, normally sombre in repose, lit up with curiosity.

'She said . . . ' began Blanco, with a cross look at Eva.

'The point is,' interrupted Eva, 'that we are stuck here until we can find someone who will take us to Venice.'

The abbess had watched their interchange with amusement. They had obviously argued many times before. She told them to wait in the courtyard and said that someone would come to show them where they were to sleep.

'This is nice, isn't it?' said Eva.

There was no reply.

'Blanco?'

'Mmm? What?'

Eva opened one eye and looked at him. She had been lying against the wall that surrounded the convent, sunning herself, delighted that she didn't have to go home just yet.

Blanco was sitting beside her on the wall and staring across the courtyard. Eva followed his gaze.

There was a novice, a trainee nun, in the courtyard. Eva knew she was a novice because her dress was a simple white shift which marked her out from the other nuns, who were all much older anyway. The novice also didn't have her hair covered and it hung halfway down her back. It was long, shiny, and luxurious and Eva couldn't help contrasting it with the tousled, untidy mop which straggled over her head and down to her shoulders. She pulled a strand out to look and its mousy blonde colour made her drop it again just as quickly. The novice in the courtyard, who looked about their age, was sitting on a bench sewing an altar cover, but every so often she would put her face up to the sun and her hair would shimmer down her back like a molten river. Blanco couldn't take his eyes from her. Eva dug him severely in the ribs.

'What?' he demanded crossly, turning to her. 'I don't think I've forgiven you yet for not telling me that we were on Malta.'

Eva opened her mouth to deny this but he interrupted her.

'And don't tell me that you didn't know,' he said. 'You didn't look in the slightest bit surprised when the abbess told us.'

'Azaz may have mentioned it,' she murmured, glancing back at the angels who were standing behind them, 'but I didn't want to worry you until I knew that he was right.'

Blanco still had his eyes firmly fixed on the novice.

'It's a bit strange,' he said, 'that we should have ended up here.'

'Remind me what happened on Malta,' said Eva.

'I know that your great-uncle stayed here for a while and that he fell in love with a woman and that he asked you to retrieve some letters which they wrote. But how did he meet her? Why are the letters so important?'

'He never told me the full story,' admitted Blanco.

Eva sighed. She was cross that Blanco was still staring into the courtyard. 'What happened to them? Why didn't he marry her? Do you think she's still here on the island?'

Blanco shrugged. 'I don't know,' he said. 'And I'm not sure that we should go looking for her either. My great-uncle is married to someone else, after all.'

'Oh,' said Eva, disappointed on both counts. She stared again at the novice who was now brushing her hair out with her fingers.

'She's not that pretty,' said Micha in Eva's ear. She and Azaz were now hovering above Eva and Blanco.

As Eva shrugged, the abbess came over to the novice and pointed at them both. Blanco immediately began to smooth down his hair and brush his tunic as surreptitiously as he could. The novice walked over to them.

'My name is Sister Agatha,' she said, smiling only at Blanco. 'The abbess has asked me to show you to the guest chamber.'

'There is one really good thing about being here,' said Eva to Micha, as she got up to follow Sister Agatha and Blanco.

'What?'

'At least the Count and the Stranger will never find us.'

Micha frowned and looked at Azaz who shrugged his shoulders.

Luca Ferron was relatively happy. He was back in his luxurious palazzo in Venice, he had virtually all the pieces of the puzzle that had eluded him for so long and all he had to do now was to translate the final part of the legend which would tell him the location of the heartstone.

Luca Ferron was an alchemist and, like all alchemists, was after a very special stone. He had first heard the legend of the heartstone decades before when he was a young man in Cordoba. He had tried to find out more about it but many people denied that it even existed and nobody knew where it was to be found. Soon the story faded into the recesses of his mind.

The memory was revived when he met Count Maleficio. They had been drawn together by their shared interest in alchemy and also because of their knowledge of the dark angel Rameel. The Count was the only other man he had ever met who had heard of the heartstone. He had heard of it years before when he had been living on the island of Malta. There, he had fallen in love with a woman who was in love with someone else. This couple had written letters to each other in code and within those letters had lain the legend of the heartstone. The Count had managed to break some of the code and was intrigued but then the other man had disappeared, with the letters. But the parts that he had translated had remained with him for years, shaping his experiments. Being able to fly like a bird and to make something that resembled thunder and lightning became his life's work.

Twenty years later, while visiting Luca Ferron in Venice, the Count had come across his love rival again, a certain Marco Polo. The Count had managed to steal the letters. Ever since then, he and Luca Ferron had been translating them.

Based on the Count's earlier work, Luca Ferron had quickly broken part of the code, which explained who could free the stone:

To win this stone the Adept must
First of all, fly like a bird,
Speak with the angels
And love like no other . . .

He had stored this in the back of his mind but, when he had met Blanco Polo and Eva di Montini at the Count's castle, he had not realized that the Adept was there, right in front of them. It had not been until Eva and Blanco had escaped from the tower that Luca understood that Eva was the one who fulfilled all the requirements. Thanks to Blanco making her sit in the flying machine, she had flown like a bird. She could definitely speak with the angels, better even than he could. And any fool could see that she was in love with Blanco.

But now, with all the letters and with virtually everything decoded, they had lost the girl and he still had to work out where the stone actually lay.

He reached for his drink and cursed. He had left it too long and the heat had gone from it. He could only drink it when it was piping hot. He could not bear it otherwise. Angrily he threw the cup against the wall and listened with satisfaction as it cracked and fell to the floor.

'You have to call me Sister Agatha,' said the novice in a soft, breathless voice, 'although I'm not really a nun. My father has only put me in here for safekeeping from the pirates until he can find me a husband. I don't really want to be here.' She had shot Blanco a very flirtatious look as she said this.

'You're in here,' she continued, turning to Eva, her smile disappearing. She motioned to a room with eight pallets in it. The one at the end had sheets folded neatly on top in a little pile. 'You can make your pallet up while I show Blanco where he is to sleep.'

She turned away and walked off before Eva could say a word. Eva narrowed her eyes as she looked after them. She didn't like that girl. Not one bit. A little spark of jealousy settled in her stomach as she watched them walk away.

That little spark grew bigger in the days that followed. Blanco hardly ever spoke to her. He was always following Sister Agatha around. She was in charge of the herb gardens and so Blanco had offered to help since they had no money to pay for the guest chamber. That was where Eva found him when she finally decided that she had to confront him.

'Blanco, I have to talk to you,' she said.

He turned round with an annoyed look on his face.

'Can't it wait?' he asked. 'Sister Agatha is showing me the properties of the lemon plant.'

'It's supposed to help guard against jealousy,' said Sister Agatha, smiling sweetly. She held out a leaf. 'Would you like to try some?'

Eva scowled at her but managed to bite back the rude reply that was hovering on the end of her tongue.

Blanco looked from her to Sister Agatha.

'We can talk later,' he said to Eva, and turned his back. Sister Agatha gave her a triumphant little smile and then turned her back too.

Eva had gazed furiously at both their backs for a moment before turning and stalking off. In addition to being annoyed, the deep dull ache somewhere in her belly region grew stronger as she realized that Blanco liked someone else better than he liked her.

A warm rush from behind made her stop.

'What's the matter?' asked Micha.

'That girl. I hate her.'

Micha looked at her sympathetically for a moment. She knew how Eva felt. She had seen how Blanco looked at Sister Agatha and she knew how much Eva liked Blanco.

'Eva!'

Eva tried to make herself as small as possible. If she could have disappeared into the wall then she would have. But she couldn't and she was soon spotted.

'There you are!' said Sister Assumpta, who was in charge of the kitchens. 'Have you found the sorrel?'

Sister Assumpta had sent her out to find some sorrel for the meat she was cooking but Eva had forgotten to ask for it when she was there and didn't want to go back.

'Oh really!' snapped Sister Assumpta when she saw the empty basket. 'I ask you to do a simple task! I'll do it myself. You go back in and scrub the carrots.'

Eva was loath to leave the comfort of Micha's wings but Sister Assumpta was staring at her and Micha herself gave her a tiny nudge. She hadn't wanted to go back to Venice but now she was thinking that she would much rather be there than on Malta.

'What are you up to?' asked Azaz, flying down to land beside Micha. She was watching Eva and she had a very calculating look on her face.

'Nothing,' she said innocently.

Azaz tried to look her in the eye but she managed to avoid him by fiddling with her wings.

'I hope you're not going to do anything to that girl,' he said.

Micha lifted her golden head and smiled. 'Me?' she said. 'Of course not.'

✱ Win your own ✱

flying machine!

Blanco Polo is determined to have his very own flying machine. And here's your chance to do the same!

What do you think the ultimate flying machine would look like?

How would it fly?

And who would pilot it?

You can design your flying machine on your own or with your friends. Perhaps your teacher might let you work on it as part of a school project.

✱ The winner will receive a specially made mini model of their flying machine ✱

Once you've designed your flying machine, send your drawings, plus your name, age and address to:

**Children's Publicity Department
Oxford University Press
Great Clarendon Street
Oxford OX2 6DP**

And we'll have them judged by one of the Red Arrows — who really do know something about flying machines!

Competition closes 30th November 2005 and judge's decision is final.
Winner(s) will be notified by post.
See www.oup.com/uk/children/angels for full terms and conditions.

HAZEL MARSHALL was born in Scotland and has lived there most of her life with occasional breaks to go travelling. She freelances for BBC Radio and enjoys learning languages and different dance styles.

Troublesome Angels and Flying Machines is Hazel's first novel and she's an author with a fresh and lively voice. An exciting new talent with a real flair for storytelling in its truest form.